MW01133394

# BOUNCE

# BOUNCE

Preston L. Allen

iUniverse, Inc.
New York  Lincoln  Shanghai

# Bounce

All Rights Reserved © 2003 by Preston L. Allen

No part of this book may be reproduced or transmitted in any form or by any means, graphic, electronic, or mechanical, including photocopying, recording, taping, or by any information storage retrieval system, without the written permission of the publisher.

iUniverse, Inc.

For information address:
iUniverse, Inc.
2021 Pine Lake Road, Suite 100
Lincoln, NE 68512
www.iuniverse.com

This is a work of fiction. Thus, names, characters, places, and incidents are either the product of the author's imagination or are used fictitiously. Any resemblance to actual persons, living or dead, events, or places is entirely coincidental. This is the Carol City, Coconut Grove, and Miami of the author's mind.

ISBN: 0-595-29871-0

Printed in the United States of America

To Dawn Arlene Mitzi,

My love and wife

Who taught me that love is greater than lust,

And that the omissions of the past

Can be redressed by the beauty and

Abundance of the present.

# C O N T E N T S

▼

## PART III

## PART IV

## PART V

## PART VI

# Acknowledgements

I keep telling people that I am not a writer of erotic fiction. Not I. I am Preston, literary writer. But I humbly admit to a personality disorder, a split personality, in fact. I am Sally Flashburn. I am a writer of erotic fiction. And I would like to thank the people who helped me with this book, even though they thought they were helping Preston, who is not here right now. The list is short because this kind of writing makes people blush. Thank you Jason, Janell, Geoffrey, Ellen, Elizabeth, Todd, Quakish. Your comments were most helpful. Thank you for reading this thing for me before it really knew where it was going. I would also like to thank the people who supported me during the writing of this book in ways too numerous to list here. Thank you Cameron, Louise, Leejay, Josett, mom, and Sally Flashburn (who is not here right now because I am Preston, literary writer).

# PART I

# BREATHE

I don't know why this is happening, but I'm thinking about mama, back before daddy left, and my little sister Mitzy Dawn, who we called Mitzy D.

I was about twelve, the oldest of all the sisters. Mitzy D was number two, which made her about ten back then. All of us were together at this chicken place in Coconut Grove (the black Grove). We used to go there after church on Sunday to eat so mama could get a break from the kitchen.

Daddy got a call on his cellphone and got up and went away from the table to go answer it where we couldn't hear. It was probably one of his ladies, but we kids didn't know about all that back then. We were just eating our chicken. And Mitzy D started choking. Mama slapped her on the back, but it didn't help. Daddy saw what was happening and ran over. He slapped her on the back, too, but it didn't help. Mitzy D was choking on a bone or something. Her mouth was opening and closing frantically, but she couldn't breath. No sound except for, huh, huhh, huhhh was coming out of her mouth. Her eyes were rolling up white in her head. She was clutching at her throat. Mama and daddy were slapping her on her back, and it was doing no good. I started to cry. Mitzy D was my favorite of all my sisters, and she was going to die. Everybody in the restaurant was looking at us, but nobody was doing anything.

This very dark-skinned Haitian man, the bus boy with a pile of dishes stacked up on a tray up on his shoulder, saw what was happening and he ran over to our table. He reached for Mitzy D, and the tray he was carrying went crashing to the ground. It sounded like a thousand dishes and glasses were breaking. Little pieces of dirty glass and ceramic chips were flying everywhere, as the Haitian man took

Mitzy D from mama and daddy and turned her around in his arms so that he was directly behind her. His arms snaked under her little armpits and he clasped his hands in the middle of her chest. He said something in his language that sounded like "Sakhaee, sakhaee," as he squeezed her chest twice. A chicken bone flew out, and Mitzy D started to scream. It was the most beautiful sound I had ever heard.

Mama and daddy were thanking the Haitian man as the manager came out and told us all of our meals were totally free. The Haitian man said he was happy to have helped and toussled Mitzy D's hair and then he and the manager stooped to clean up the broken glasses and plates, and soon everything was almost back to normal in the restaurant. Everybody was eating except for me and Mitzy D. She didn't have an appetite anymore. She was just looking down at her plate, breathing, breathing, happy to be breathing. And I was holding her hand and telling her, "I was so scared. You should've seen your eyes. Girl, I was so afraid you were gonna die." Then when we were in the car, mama started complaining to daddy.

"Look at her dress. How is that ever gonna come out, huh? That Haitian messed up her good white dress with his dirty hands."

Daddy looked in the back where Mitzy D was leaning against me, breathing, breathing, taking in deep, deep breaths. He said to mama, "You crazy. That Haitian saved her life."

"But who's gonna clean that dress?"

"Stop talking like that. Do you hear what you're saying in front of the children?"

"Don't you tell me to shut up. Who are you? Do you clean? Do you do any work around the house? Me. I have to clean that dress. People who don't clean got some nerve telling people who do all the cleaning to shut up."

"Do you hear yourself? Be thankful she's alive."

"I am thankful. She's my daughter. I carried her nine months. Don't tell me I'm not thankful. But look what he did to her dress. You never take us to any-place classy. In a classy place, his hands would have been clean."

"In a classy place she would have choked to death. Is that what you want?"

"Don't play no word games with me. I love my children. I take good care of them. You see how good I take care of them. I slave over them. Whatever they become is because of me. Don't you dare talk to me like that. Where are you? What do you do? Do you clean? Don't try to make me look like a fool. I know what I'm talking about."

"Dammit," daddy said, "I'll clean her damned dress when we get home."

"I'd like to see that."

"I'll do it!"

"To make me look like a fool. You clean one dress all year. I clean every day. Like hell I'm gonna let you clean that dress. I'm not gonna let you touch that dress. I'll clean it when I get home like I clean everything else."

Daddy, who was driving, groaned, "I'm just saying, be happy she's alive. Damn. Damn."

"Stop cursing in front of the children."

"Be happy!"

"I am happy! Shut up!"

My little sister, Mitzy Dawn Sanders, rested against my shoulder, breathing deep lusty breaths.

# The Master

Cindique Sanders-Lassiter
April 16
Miami, Florida

Those were the good old days, before the ball started to bounce.
Hard.

I don't know why I'm thinking about it when I should be dialing this damned phone trying to make some money.

I don't know why.

But that's the way it begins, this story of love and lies and life, which like a big red ball of fun bounces. With a bounce! A mama, a sister, a chicken bone. Now let me tell you how it ends. With a bounce!

It bounces. I bounce.

It bounces.

The customers, I mean, why does my call sheet have to have all of the duds? Is this a plan? Another curse out, don't call back, I'm not interested, hanging up before I can get into my spiel good?

I shake my head at my empty tally sheet and sigh. But there's sweet music going on around me. I push the headphones off and swivel to Red Redd, who has a live one.

They're all live ones for him. Red Redd is the master.

"Can you dream big? Can you dream real big? Yes? Then what I want you to do for me, for both of us, is to take out your checkbook. Go ahead and get it. I'll wait for you."

While he waits for the live one to return with a checkbook, Red writes something on the edge of his spiel sheet. I crane my neck to see. A number, 230, preceded by double dollar signs. His commission if he closes this sale. *When* he closes this sale. I smile encouragement at him, my colleague. He shoots back smugness. The master don't need nobody's smile. The master know how good he is. Does he know how good he looks in his Michael Jordan jersey?

Red Redd swivels his back to me because the live one has returned.

"—Okay. You got your checkbook? Now I want you to look carefully at the first check in that checkbook. Are you looking? Good. Now I want you to tell me what the check number is. 2315? Good. Now I want you to fill out check number 2315 with this amount. Three thousand two-hundred seventy-two. Did you get that? Did you write it down? Are you liquid for that amount? Good. Then write it down. You wrote it down? Good. Now what I'm gonna do for you, for both of us, is send our runner over to pick up check number 2315, and then the deal will be sealed. You will be well on your way to realizing your dreams of untold wealth. Can you dream it? Can you dream it? Well, we're gonna make it real."

The brother has a voice like a televangelist. Take my sins away, brother.

"Another one! You're so good."

"Shut up," says Red, putting a hand over his mouthpiece. "Get back to work before Groan of Arc fires your ass." He rolls his eyes and goes back to the live one.

I frown him a good one, but he doesn't see it. Bounce. Bounce. Back to my headphones, back to my call sheets. Byron Miller, Luis Millien, Chuck Wagner Milner, III. Who are these people? More duds. It's no use. I push my feet back into my mules and get up and peep out the entrance of our cubicle. Most of the lights on the floor are off. The cleaning lady's pushing a cart full of mops and spritzers down the aisle, stopping to empty our plastic garbage pails of their coffee cups, soda cans, and crumpled call sheets. It's almost nine. All the other phone pros have gone home. Groan of Arc's in her office tallying the day's sales. The sliver of light from her partially opened door streams out onto the darkened floor. The only ones left in the sales room are me, the cleaning lady, and the master who, amazingly, is in the middle of another call.

"—but can you dream it? Can you really dream it?"

The brother got passion. The brother got devotion. The brother need a girl to share the motion lotion. I elbow the back of his head and giggle when he loses his rhythm. He clamps his hand over the mouthpiece and says, "Now see? That's why you ain't makin no money, Cindique."

I pucker up and peck him on the forehead. "You're no fun."

"I'm working."

I'm about to say something else, something playful to him, but he's paying me no mind, and nature's calling. I collect my blank tally sheet and drop it in the daily tally slot on the way to the powder room. I take care of business in there. Take a hit of a joint, too. (Confession is good for the soul.) Then I head back to the cubicle to say goodnight and discover that Groan of Arc, with her short-skirt-wearing ass, is there.

Locked in a tender kiss with the master.

I duck into an empty cubicle and put my hand over my mouth to stifle the naw, naw, naws trying to burst out on a wave of giggles. Now let me see if I got this right. Groan of Arc, our boss, is married with a pair of twin sons who play tennis or some sport up at college she's always bragging about. Red Redd, on the other hand, lives with some girl named Tawana, and they have a little brown skinned boy whose picture is tacked up in the cubicle, looking all cute just like his daddy. Red is my age, maybe a little older than me. He can't be more than twenty-five. But I know he's younger than fifty, or however old it is that Groan of Arc (Mrs. Joan Darcy, our boss, let me remind you) is. And not that it matters, but Groan of Arc is white, and Red Redd, despite being red-boned with freckles and gray eyes, is black.

It's so juicy my heart can't help but race. Red and Groan. Naw, naw, naw.

I keep my ears open for signs that their stolen moment has ended. They have to know I'm somewhere in the building, but that's the way love is. It makes you do stupid things that get you caught. Anyway, they're quick about it. Relatively speaking. When I hear the click clack of Groan of Arc's stiletto heels moving off down the hall, I count ten Mississippis and then stroll back to the cubicle, all la-dee-da. The master is back on the phone. This time it's his baby's mama, Tawana.

"—yeah, I'ma work late, I'm on a roll. I made 695 dollars today. I'ma stay late and try to get it up to at least a thousand. So I could put a down payment on that car for you…yeah…you know I'ma do it, because I love you so much…Lexus, beemer, Mercedes, whatever you want. Can you dream it? I'll make your dream come true, baby, you know I will—." Meanwhile he's scribbling on his spiel sheet. *Think positive. Think positive. Think positive.*

I'm sitting on the desk with my legs crossed. Showing my pretty knees. Checking him out. The shaved head, the loop of gold in each ear, a cluster of four cinnamon flakes on each cheek, the pretty eyes. The tears falling from his eyes. He brushes them away, but too late. Red clamps a hand over the mouth-piece and frowns up at me: "You ain't gone yet?"

"I'm waiting for you."

"What! Get out of here, girl."

"The parking lot is scary at night. Everybody already went home."

"You're crazy. Ain't nothin gonna happen to you out there."

"Where's Groan of Arc? Did she leave, yet?" I say, all la-dee-da.

Our eyes lock. He looks away.

"Where is Groan?"

"I don't know." Looking kinda shamed now. Kinda biting his lip. He goes back to his call. Mumbling. "—just my co-worker. She's crazy. She wants me to walk her out to her car, or something. She's scared. Lemme go do this. She's crazy. I'll call you back."

He puts down the phone and rises, long and lean, looming over me, in his loose shirt and over-sized pants. I try to communicate to him with my eyes, but he is clueless. We walk to the door with him a step behind me, doing his 2 cool 4 U walk. In the elevator ride down, he keeps to his side of the box while I face the numbers, struggling to keep the giggles in check. Red and Groan. My, oh my. We do not talk until I reach into my purse.

"You want a cigarette?"

"No smoking in the elevator."

"I know that. I mean for later."

He doesn't answer. He's no fun.

Outside in the parking lot, two of the pole-mounted lamps are burnt out. It *is* dark, but not scary. I have no fear of the dark anymore. Now that I am free and single again, the dark is beautiful to me, a time to hang loose, a time to celebrate, a time to bounce, bounce, bounce. When we get to my Toyota, I pull out the keys and begin to fumble with them deliberately. I have to find a way to tell Red the thing I've lured him out here for. As I fool with my keys, he smirks. He must think I'm really as crazy as he told Tawana. *It's just Cindique, my crazy co-worker.*

"Red," I say to him.

"What?" Smirking.

"Red."

In a sudden move, he backs me up against the car and puts his arms on either side of me. I'm trapped against his chest, locked into his mischievous eyes. The smell of him is intense. Lavender something, sweet something, something pungent, man musk. It's real nice. He brings his face down close to mine. All confident. All proud. Smirking. "What?" he says.

"I saw you cry."

He backs away.

"I wasn't crying."

"I saw you."

"I had something in my eye."

"Tears."

"I gotta go."

"You have pretty eyes."

"Bye, Cindique."

"With your cute ass."

He shoves his hands in his pockets, drawing back up his baggy pants which had slipped too low on his hips. "I'm outta here."

I watch him walk away, none of those 2 cool 4 U strides this time, but heavy steps. "Red, the master, Roderick Redd. Thanks for walking me to the car," I holler after him, feeling bad about it. I didn't mean to hurt his feelings. Didn't mean to shame him. There's too much shame in this big red bouncing ball already.

"Red, I'm sorry!"

He doesn't turn, doesn't answer, as he shoulders open the door.

"Big boys don't cry, Red."

He disappears inside the building and the door closes after him. I stick the key in the door of the Toyota. Then I turn suddenly and peer up at the offices where we work. A face, Groan of Arc's, withdraws quickly from the window, and the last light on the fourth floor blinks off.

The master has a master.

It's too funny for words.

On the way home, I keep thinking about it. In the three weeks I've been at McDarc Investments, I've seen her husband exactly once, a tall, elegantly dressed man with steel gray hair and piercing blue eyes. Strikingly handsome, in a white man sort of way. Alexandros. He's the one with the money. McDarc Investments is only one of many businesses that Alexandros Darcy owns. McDarc Investments, a company that sells nothing but dreams, is only one of his many scams. The city commissioners, the ones he hasn't bribed, are constantly trying to shut us down.

Red. Groan. Alexandros? A triangle.

Naw, naw, naw.

# THE KEYS TO MY...

I open the door to the small apartment on the top floor of the ancient, but afford-able apartment building. It's not in the worst area of Miami, but it's not in the best either. Considering my tight budget, I like to think that my place is a cozy, nicely decorated space. There's the porcelain vase I fill daily with fresh yellow roses. I love roses in all colors, but yellow is my favorite. To add interest, there are my throw pillows placed about the living room in alternating red, white, and checked patterns. There are some homey touches, too, with my hand-sewn cur-tains and self-upholstered couches. Like my mama, I am good with my hands. But this is not going to be a good night because a light is on, and I never leave the lights on.

At the edge of the carpet near the door, are Tyrone's shoes, the heavy work boots, too highly polished to really be work boots. He never gave back his key. I never changed the lock. I had convinced myself that he's not like that. That he's many things, but not that. Yet here he is now, up in my place.

Stupid. Stupid. Bounce. Bounce.

I find him in the bedroom sitting on my bed. A basket brown man with wild-man naps, a thick neck and lips, and wide-spaced, long-lashed, light brown eyes that never seem to get it. All of my drawers are open, my possessions thrown about. My filing cabinet's open, too, and the folders dumped out. The room is a mess. Tyrone holds up two photographs to his face. One is of me and Jake in fishing gear showing off the marlin we had caught. In the other, I am kissing Jake on the mouth. Before I can begin to explain a thing I have no need to explain because, one, Jake was before Tyrone, two, Jake had nothing to do with why me and Tyrone broke up, and three, those photographs are my private property—but before I can explain all this that I have no real obligation to explain, but will as a courtesy to set an ex's heart and mind at ease, Tyrone has sprung from the bed and boxed me a hard one on the ear. It sends me sprawling backwards and down. Physically and emotionally.

Tyrone comes and squats his bulk over me, pushing the photographs in my face, demanding, "Who dis?"

I hold back my tears. My fear of the dark. "Get out of here. Gimme back my key."

"Who dis?" He pushes the Polaroids against my mouth. I clench it closed tight. He tries to pull it open. I am resisting him. He is strong. He pulls my mouth open with his strong hands, strong fingers and pushes one of the Polaroids inside, hard, scraping up the inside of my gums real good. I'm fighting him, gagging, trying to bite his fingers. Tyrone's laughing. He puts the other Polaroid in his breast pocket and gets up from over me, tapping the pocket with the picture in it. "I'm gonna find him. Believe dat."

I spit out photograph and fire: "Get out of my house. Gimme back my key."

"Who is he?"

"None of your damned business. Get out of my house!" The walls are thin. Someone will hear. Someone always hears. I am shouting. He clamps a hand over my mouth and grabs my hair, which he had always loved because it falls to my shoulders easy in white girl waves.

"Don't be yelling at me. You forget who I am?"

He drags me up by my hair and walks me backwards with his face pressed against mine. His face is sweaty. Clammy. He smells bad. Despite his wildman hair (carefully groomed wildman hair), he is really a neat freak and particular about hygiene. He has always been picky about smell. Something must have really set him off. "You're gonna tell me who he is." He walks me backwards, to where I remember seeing the scissors. I fight against him, but not enough to make him change his mind or his direction. We are reflected in the full-length closet mirror. The way he is holding me, the way I am clawing him, it looks like some crazy, intense dance. "You're gonna tell me his name. You're gonna tell me where he live at. You're gonna tell me how good he fuck you." He walks me backwards until I can't walk anymore because I'm pressed against the wall next to the high bureau. I reach without seeing to where the scissors had been. My fingers curl around them. They are the sturdy kind, good for cutting stubborn burlap to make interesting curtains out of. "—you're gonna tell me about his dick, how long it was, how good it was—." I plunge the scissors into the flesh of his armpit because I have read that that is a very tender area. He jumps back howling, clutching at the wound. I lunge at him again and catch him in the thigh. Bright red spreads over his jeans. It looks like some new crazy sort of style. He staggers backwards. Flops down on the bed. Both hands clamped around the cut leg. Groaning. I retreat to the far wall to watch him bleed. "You stabbed me," he says. "I'm gonna whup yo ass."

I hold up the scissors in warning.

"Look whachu did my leg."

"Gimme my key back."

He's bleeding all over the bedspread I sewed with my own hands. "Get me something to clean this up. Ow. Ow. Help me clean dis. Lookit dis mess."

It is a mess.

"Then you gotta leave. You gotta leave my house and give my key back."

In the chaos on the floor, I rescue a beach towel and toss it to him. I back into the bathroom, keeping an eye on him, and dig through the cabinet until I find the peroxide bottle, which I fling at him. Then I fling the alcohol bottle at him, too. He pulls off his shirt and splashes the alcohol on the sliced flesh under his arm. He looks up, and I am amazed. There is a grin on his face. "You gotta help me with dis." Wincing. Grinning. "Come here."

"You're gonna try to grab me."

"Come here and help me. I can't do it by myself."

"You hit me."

"You used to love me." He's getting up. Grinning.

"I swear to god, Tyrone, I'll kill you—!" I back up to the wall and hold the scissors out in front of me. "Stay away from me!"

"Okay. Okay." His eyes. They don't get it. He has no shirt on his hairless barrel chest. He has a bloody towel wadded under his arm. His jeans have a scarlet leg. This is love? Doesn't he get it? I go in the living room and open the door and kick his pretty boots out the door. Eventually, he limps out of the bedroom. I give him a wide berth to pass through the open front door. Gone is the grin. But his eyes. He just doesn't get it. He shakes his head sadly as he passes. Dragging himself through the door. I slam it shut after him. Turn off the lights. Sink down to the floor. Release the tears. About fifteen minutes later, there is a knock at the door.

"Cindique!" One voice.

"Cindique! Cindique!" Another voice. The walls are thin. Somebody has heard. Somebody always hears. Somebody always comes. Somebody always comes too late. It is the neighbors. The Puerto Rican lesbian who said she would help with the rent if I let her eat me. Rose, Rosa, Rosita, Rosie? And her room-mate, Nicole, Nikki, Nike, Nikita, who might not be gay because she has never hit on me. Plus, I think she has a baby. Then again, you never know.

"Cindique, you all right?"

"I'm fine."

Through the door. "We heard sounds."

"I'm fine. He's gone."

"We didn't hear him leave."

"He left quietly."

"We could go get the landlord's key and come in and check, you know?"

"He's gone, I promise you."

"You want us call somebody for you? Your mom?"

"Hell no."

"*Ay pobrecita!* Cindique, we're here for you. We don't see no lights on in there. Is he holding you hostage?"

"Look down on the ground. See the blood? That's his blood."

"Oh snap. Look at the blood," one says.

"She got his ass good."

"Oh snap. Good for you, Cindique. Good for you."

"Yeah. Go home. I'm fine." Gossiping bitches. Now they have something to gossip about. She got his ass good. Yeah. And he still has my key. I sit in the dark with my back against the door and the scissors in my hand facing my handiwork. (My curtains look good framing a window full of stars.) Now I have something else to add to tomorrow's crowded itinerary, pay my late cable bill, get my oil changed, change the lock on my door, get my phone turned back on.

Cry.

# SLUT. MA'AM.

So I get to work the next day an hour and a half late. Groan of Arc calls me into her office to chew me out, I assume. But that's not how she is. She'll chew you out right in public. In her office, she tells me to take a seat, and I plop down on the stool across from her. The arched eyebrows, tanned skin, shining raven-black hair, thin ochre-painted lips that neither smile nor frown. Really, she's a good looking woman. Exotic looking. But severe. Her eyebrows are arched too high. Her nose is too long, too lean. She is drinking coffee. She pours me a cup. Napkin. Stirrer. Styrofoam cup.

She holds out a creamer. "You like cream?"

"I like it dark."

"Fine." Missing the joke. She drops the creamer packet back in the silver server and places her hands palm down on the desk. Her fingers are long and lean, too. She has a French manicure. Her hands are beautiful. Her words are like cold water icing your body unexpectedly when you turn on the shower: "You're the one who started calling me Groan of Arc."

"No," I shake my head, lying my ass off. "I never called you that."

"You were late again."

"—I called in. I had some emergencies that came up."

"Your sales are poor. You can make more money flipping hamburgers."

"Mrs. Darcy, I need this job."

"You're too good for us. Too good for a 350-a-week draw plus commission."

"Mrs. Darcy," I stutter, touching the left side of my face, which has swollen, "my husband beat me up last night."

"Oh my."

"He had been following me. He said he saw me talking to Roderick in the parking lot after work last night. Roderick is my friend, that's all."

It is not exactly the truth, and she is not exactly buying it. Unsmiling. Unfrowning. Her pretty nails drumming the desk. I choke up to cry.

"Tissue?"

I sniffle. "Yes."

She plucks the baby-powder scented sheets from a silver cache next to her phone and deposits them in my palm. She clears her throat. She shuffles paper. She hems. She haws. She begins, "Men are…." She pre-empts her lecture with another hem. A haw. She looks me straight in the eye. "Cindique," she says, "I'm going to give you one more week to pick up your sales. Business is business. Men are…a problem…I'm sure you know that." She indicates one particular man with a slight nod to the door. Beyond the door. Red, she seems to be saying. Red. And I am imaging them together. The difference in age. The difference in skin. I see her bent over, in one of those hip-hugging mini skirts she's always wearing. I see him taking her from behind, that mini skirt flipped up over her plump little square-shaped butt. She's wearing tall heels as usual, and her long, skinny, perfectly-tanned, old-lady legs bend slightly forward at the knees as she takes her pleasure. The look on her face is…naw, naw, naw. She knows that I know, and she is embarrassed, as two slender fingers come up to hide her lips. Her eyes are still smiling. Blushing. Her eyes are asking, this is embarrassing, I know, but we do have an understanding, don't we? Don't we? Now she is touching her bottom lip with the tip of one finger. She wants to lick that finger. She is saying, "But, well, we can't let our emotions interfere with our work. Most men are able to separate the two—we must learn to do it too if we are to play their game. Do you understand me, Cindique?"

I move the tissue away from my face. "Yes."

"Do you?"

"Pick up my sales?" (Leave Red alone? I can do that.)

"One week."

"One week. I can do it. I know I can." (And don't be calling you Groan of Arc anymore?) "I know I can."

"I know you can. You have potential."

"Thanks for seeing my potential." (Thank you for not firing me. Thank you, thank you, thank you, Joan of Darkness.)

(Slut.) (Ma'am.)

The world is a big red bouncing ball of fun.
Bounce. Bounce.

# PERSISTENCE

It has always been professional and platonic between Red and me, despite my flirting. But last night he tried to kiss me. *After* I had seen his tears. Maybe there's a connection. Maybe it's a man thing. Kinda like what I learned through my years with Tyrone. A man who shows weakness must compensate with strength. Sexual aggressiveness. Violence. Or maybe Red's just suddenly realized how gorgeous his cubicle mate is. In my weakened condition, yeah, I can accept that. I am gorgeous. I really am, you know? The smooth complexion and straight hair texture from my mama's roots in the Dominican Republic. The almond eyes, thick lips, and sexy curves from my daddy's folk up in Georgia. Yeah, I got a little meat on me. I am fleshy, but fine. And today Red is all over me. He's moved his chair closer to mine. He's made excuses to reach across my chest to get things, brushing against me on the sly. He's put his phone down to give me tips on selling. Oooh.

"When you got a live one, you'll know, because they'll be asking questions. The duds just agree with everything you say. They're just wasting your time. They're just waiting to hang up on you. You could almost hear 'em in the background painting their toenails or something. A good phone pro listens for the inquiring mind. That's how we know. That's how we get 'em."

"Uh hum. I think I understand."

He's holding my hand, and I'm only half enjoying it because I'm looking around to see if Joan of Darkness is hovering nearby. When her door opens, I push my chair a safe distance away from him. Wouldn't you know it? Here she comes, sauntering over on spindly heels that make her legs look long and skinny.

"How are you all doing?" Her hand on Red's shoulder. Platonic. (Yeah, right.) "Making any money?"

"Making money for the man," Red says. Embarrassed.

"Making money for the man," I say without looking up.

"Don't forget to make money for the woman, too." It's a joke. She laughs. Red laughs. I am late to laugh. But then I laugh too loud. She looks at me strange, then slinks away, unsmiling, unfrowning, on spindly heels.

Red starts back to teaching me about selling. But his voice has changed. Somber now. "It's like this, Cindique. I make it look easy, but it ain't about skill, really. Skill is good. Skill helps. Skill improves your chances. But the real key to selling, selling anything, is persistence."

"Persistence," I say, taking his hand in mine.

He's looking down at our united palms and fingers and smiling a sad smile. "The more selling you do, the more likely someone will buy. The guy who trained me called it the rule of one in ten. If the average salesman talks to ten clients, one will buy, no matter how good or how bad the salesman or the product is. I mean, look at us. Look at the crap we're selling. What is this? What is this really? Nobody gets rich off what we sell. We're lying to people. A bad, obvious lie. And still they buy. Some of 'em."

"Red."

"What?"

"Why were you crying yesterday?"

He shrugs and he has this helpless look on his face. "My life is screwed."

"Mine is, too."

"Not like mine."

"My ex-husband beat me up last night."

"You were married? At your age?"

"So? You got a baby *at your age*. You got your sweet little Tawana."

"Not anymore. She has a boyfriend."

"Really?"

"She doesn't live with me anymore. She hardly even lets me see my boy. She—." We look up at the same time, and Joan of Darkness has spindly-walked back to us, almost catching us holding hands.

"I see you two haven't been very productive today. Still gabbing, huh? Well, there's a solution to that. Cindique, since you're so interested in getting your sales up, I'm moving you to a new cubicle."

"But—," I start to protest.

She clicks her French-manicured nails on my empty tally sheet and says, "Do you have a problem with that, Cindique?" Unsmiling. Unfrowning.

"No."

So I am moved to a cubicle with a girl even chubbier than myself. Gertha Sedansky. Bushy eyebrows. Square shoulders. Dungarees and a shiny cowboy-themed belt buckle. We don't talk at all. We have nothing to talk about. I don't want her cupcakes. She doesn't want mine. Her voice is a high-pitched whine as she reads her spiel. I follow Red's advice about the rule of one in ten. I call and I call, reading the spiel mechanically, and I get my first sale in three days. Then my second. Soon I have three. My tally sheet reads $540 when Gertha gets up to leave and I realize what time it is. The other phone pros have gone home. The cleaning lady is pushing her cart down the aisles. Half the lights are turned off. I pull off my headphones and hear the voice of the master, who is still hard at work: "—but can you dream it? Can you really dream it?"

Joan of Darkness is in her office. As I pass her open door, I see that her sexy shoes are off and she's rubbing one stockinged foot propped up on the stool in front of her chair. Long day. How elegant.

I complete a deliberately noisy trip to the powder room, then peep out the door. Here comes boss lady padding down the aisle in her nylons. Ducking into Red's cubicle. I go to the toilet and fill it with clump after clump after clump of toilet paper. He has a baby. He has a girlfriend. Damn it, leave him alone. I flush the toilet and its contents spill out onto the floor.

I burst out of the bathroom hollering, "The toilet's spilling over! The toilet's spilling over!"

# THE BITCH

I know that my phone's been turned back on because it's ringing when I open the door. I pick up. It's Tyrone.

"You something else. You is something else."

"Bye, Tyrone."

"You ain't even wonder why I came by yesterday."

"You needed me to hem your pants."

"You really something else."

"Did I do a good job? How do they fit? Did I hem your sleeves good too?"

"You wouldn't be sayin that if I was over there."

"Bye, Tyrone. Say hi to your wife."

"That bitch done gone."

"Oooh."

"You is my wife. Once married, always married. The Bible say you can't be divorced from your first love."

"Aw, hell naw. Don't go there."

"The Lord only recognize one marriage. Me and you's gonna be husband and wife in heaven."

"Is that your plan, Tyrone? To get me back when we go to heaven?"

"That is my plan."

"Then I ain't going to heaven."

"Fresh mouth girl."

"I ain't going anywhere you are. Bye, Tyrone."

"Mama died."

That one gets me. That one deflates me. I sink down to the couch. "...the cancer?"

"Yeah."

"When?"

"This morning. About four in the morning. Tha's why I was over there last night. She sent me. She wanted to see you before she died. She was askin for you right down to the end. You know she loved you. You know she loved you..."

"...yes, yes."

"...how she loved you."

"...yes."

I remember the love.

And the guilt.

—for not calling Mrs. Lassiter, not even once after the divorce. For keeping the calls brief and shallow when Mrs. Lassiter had called me dutifully once a month. For taking the money that she sent on my birthdays, for Christmas, for Easter, and whenever after a brief, shallow monthly phone call that she suspected (correctly) that I was in another of my dire financial straits. Yes. Yes. I am empty, empty, and the tears are rolling off my cheeks for Mrs. Lassiter, my seventh grade teacher, whose asshole class clown son Tyrone I had married.

"Why didn't you just say that? Why didn't you just tell me, Tyrone? Why the hell you had to go through my stuff?"

"—I was sittin there in your house waitin. I was thinkin about how much I miss you. How I had made a big mistake lettin you go. Everything I done did to you."

"—You should've just told me. I loved her. Damn you, Tyrone. Damn you. You're always fuckin up my life. Shit. Shit. Shit."

"—That day I walked out—"

"—When's the funeral?'

"—day I walked out on you, I don't know what I was thinkin. I was thinkin you so smart and I'm so stupid, I mean, damn, I didn't even pass my own mama's class. Damn, how dumb can you be, right? I mean, why should I be good? I know what the Bible says, but it was just too much pressure. A man who had to turn to his mama to take care of his wife, a man who knew his wife musta been laughing at him behind his back. Too much pressure. Shit. It was just too much pressure—."

"—Where they having the wake at? Tyrone, listen to me, shut up. Shut up. Where they having the wake at? At Aunti Gina's house?"

"—too much pressure to be good, and smart, and dumb, and a man, and faithful."

"What did you say?"

"Huh?"

"Is that why you cheated?"

"Is *what* why I cheated?"

Bounce.

"Tyrone," I say, "now you know I don't like it when you don't listen to me. You talk too damn much, you don't listen enough. That's your problem. You don't listen."

"I'm listening now," he says. "Baby."

"I ain't your baby. I ain't never gonna be your baby again."

"We'll see about dat."

"Tyrone, I hate you. You know that, right?"

"No, you don't."

"Yes, I do. I hate you very much," I say. "But that's cool because I still need to know where they're holding your mama's wake at."

"You gonna sit with me at the wake?"

"Nope."

"You gonna talk with me?"

"Nope."

"You gonna tell me who the man in the picture is?"

"Hell no."

"Did you fuck him while we was married?"

I decide to answer that one. I know how his mind works. And I am angry: "I fucked him before we were married. And a whole lot after."

He is quiet for a while. Thinking it through. Too quiet.

"Tyrone?"

"How soon after?"

"That first night."

"That *same* night?"

"No, not that night…we were kissing a lot because I was tense. He had to calm me down first with the kissing and the feeling up. Then he got the KY and gave me anal, which doesn't count as fucking in the natural sense of the word. By the time he stuck it in the coochie, it was after midnight, so no, it was not that same night, technically, because it was after midnight."

"You a bitch, you know that? A bitch."

"Where's your mama's wake, Tyrone?"

There is sniffling amid the cursing.

"Where's your mama's wake, Tyrone?"

"Bitch!" he says, bawling like the big baby he is. "I ain't tellin you nothin. I don't want you at my mama's wake."

"If I really wanted to go, I could just call Aunti Gina! Your mama wouldn't want me at her wake. She would want me far, far away from you. You big dummy! I hate you!"

Tyrone hangs up the phone like the big baby he is. Big dummy. Big hypocrite. He can cheat on me as many times as he wants, and I'm supposed to just deal with it. Then he gets upset because I get a little piece *after* he dumps me. Did he expect me to wait there and pine away for him?

I'm independent. I'm in control. I'm empowered. Who needs a loser like Tyrone?

Fuck him.

# BUT REALLY...

I did pine.

Bounce.

I kept believing he would come back.

Bounce. Bounce.

He was bad but he was my bad and I missed him and I hated the girl who took him, skinny little crack pipe bitch....

But you know what? I got over it.

Mrs. Lassiter told me to get over it. She called me once a month to tell me how lucky I was to be away from a no-good bum like her son.

And I kept the calls brief and shallow.

I wish I really had slept with someone the night Tyrone dumped me. I wish I had. I did call Jake. I really would have slept with Jake. He was so sweet. He was so kind. He's the only one I would have allowed to get close to me after the hurt, but he was married by then. I wish it hadn't taken me a year to date again. I should have slept with someone. I wish I had slept with someone, not counting the lesbian, because that was a mistake.

Rose, Rosa, Rosita, Rosie.

I should have taken Mrs. Lassiter's advice. I shouldn't have gotten married at 15. Three years with Tyrone. Two years on my own.

I am 20.

# MRS. JOAN DARCY

But now it is too dangerous to stay. The next day, I travel to work with the scissors in my purse. I go into the office to see Joan, to tell her that today is my last day. To tell her that I have stayed up all night packing. That I have informed my landlady of my intent to break my lease. My plan is to move upstate, but I will need a job.

"—And I know you guys have a branch up there. It would be great if you could tell them that I'm a hard worker and that I'd be an asset. I know I can do the job. I know I can do it. I have to get out of here. My husband is going to kill me. I know it."

Joan shakes her head. "You're so young. Poor child, how did you get yourself into such a mess?"

"I don't know."

She reaches across the desk and takes my hands in hers. She has a sweet look on her face. "I'll make the call. Don't you worry about it. When are you leaving?"

"Tonight. Tomorrow. No later than day after tomorrow."

This seems to please her, and she says, "If you need a place to stay until you leave, we have a small guest house on our estate that you are free to use."

Talk about surprise. "Thank you, Mrs. Darcy! I don't know what to say."

She clasps my hands tighter. Her face becomes less severe. She is not the slut now. She is a friend. "We had a daughter. She took up with a man. It wasn't bad enough that he was shiftless and domineering, and probably abusive, but he had to control her mind, too. She followed him to this religious commune he was a part of. My husband tried to keep track, but these people were off the radar. We even had her kidnapped one time, but she went back. It was the man…he had this control over her. He called us a month after she died. *A month.* She had practically starved to death. He told us she was in heaven. My husband and I haven't been the same since."

I reach to embrace her, but I guess she doesn't need it. She rolls backwards in her chair and resumes her usual rigidity. "I'll have the help prepare the guest house for you. You can take today off to finalize whatever affairs you may have."

"Thank you, Mrs. Darcy." I have to call the movers or rent a van. I have to find a cheap storage rental for my things. I have to get my deposits back from the phone and electric companies. I will need a place to stay when I get up there. I have to call my cousin upstate to see if she'll let me crash until I find a place. "I do have a lot of stuff to take care of before I leave."

"I thought as much. I'm so glad I can help." She beams. "And perhaps Roderick Redd would lend you a hand if we asked him. He's made enough commission the past couple days, he can afford the time away from the phones. He's your friend. Would it be helpful if I asked him for you?"

"Yes."

(Bounce.)

# PART II

# MORE PLEASE

We take his car, a white Ford Bronco with over-sized whitewall tires, leather seats, a slammin stereo system. He kisses my hand as we pull out of the parking lot. It sends a little shiver through me. I glance up to the fourth floor window, but there is no face peering out of it. This does not mean that she does not see. This does not mean that she isn't watching us from some other part of the building, Joan Darcy, my new best, generous friend. I do not want her to see us. It would be wrong for her to see us. I would feel pretty crappy if she saw us. The bass from his stereo is thumping, our heads are bumping, and he holds my hand, as I give him directions to my building and rationalize that he is *not* her husband. He is her secret thing. Big difference. She has no claim on him.

"You packed up the bed yet?" he says.

"No, but I stripped off the sheets."

"You're gonna have to put 'em back on. I don't want you to get mattress burns."

"Oooh. I think I remember what box I packed them in."

He kisses my hand, he kisses my arm, he kisses my neck. The boldness. The overcompensation. I know what he's going through. He is all man now.

And I am all with it.

The driver beside us honks her horn, and Red rights the swerving Bronco, laughing. I warn, playfully, "You better watch where you going. Don't want to get in no accident."

"Whachu like, baby?" Kissing my neck again.

"Watch the road."

"I'm watching you." Kiss neck. Kiss neck. "Whachu like?"

"I like romance."

"Foreplay?"

"I like foreplay."

"I give lots." Kiss neck. Kiss neck. Swerve to safety. Kiss neck. "What's sensitive about you?"

"Me? I don't like to be picked at."

"No." Kiss neck. Kiss neck. "What part of you is sensitive?"

"All parts."

"Be specific."

"Neck."

"Uh huh." Kiss neck. Kiss neck. Swerve.

"Damn! Please don't kill us."

"Master of the road. Me." Kiss neck. Kiss neck. "More parts please."

"Face."

"Where?"

"Eyes. Lips. Ears."

"Check. Check. Check. More please. Be specific."

"The obvious."

"Name it." Kiss eyes. Kiss ears. Kiss lips. "Name please?"

"Breasts, of course."

"Where?"

"Nipple."

"Where?"

"Where? The whole thing."

"Tip? Cylinder? Aureole?" Kiss neck. Kiss neck.

"Tip."

"Check. Can I see?"

"No!"

"Let me see it please."

"Red, this is a very interesting side of you. I've never seen you like this before."

"Show please."

I open the buttons on my blouse. Give him a peek of Victoria's Secret Angel Bra. Silky, silky chocolate skin. "There."

He smiles his approval. "Show nipple now."

"No. We're driving."

"Correction. I'm driving. You're sitting. Show please."

"Then you do it, funny man."

"I'm driving. Safety first. Show nipple please."

Down goes my D-cup. What he sees there sobers him up real good like I knew it would.

"Pretty…damn pretty," losing his crazy voice.

My breasts are big, with nipples like fat, ripe fruit. The aureoles are very black in contrast to the rest of the flesh and they spread their circles over the brownish peaks like large, black coins. My breasts have always been beautiful that way.

"Damned pretty. Damn, damn, damn pretty." Approving smile. Leaning over. Kissing nipple. Horns blare. We swerve.

"That was close."

Back to his crazy voice: "More parts please."

"Come on, Red. Wait until we get home."

"More parts." Kiss nipple. Lick nipple. Greedy lick. Long suckle. "More parts please."

"Small of back. Just above the crack."

"Yum. Tattoo there? Tattoo I bet."

"I'll surprise you."

"No surprise. Tell now please." Kiss nipple. Kiss nipple.

"Yes. There is a tattoo there."

"Butterfly? Snake?"

"Rose."

"Yum. More parts." Kiss nipple. Kiss nipple. Long suckle. Free hand caresses thigh. "More parts please."

"The coochie."

"Where?"

"Everywhere! It's the coochie."

"Be specific."

"Inside. Outside. Pubic hair. Clit."

"Especially clit?" Free hand under skirt. Fingers on clit. I'm shifting my knees. Kiss nipple. Kiss nipple.

"Yes. Especially."

"Especially here?"

"Uhh. Uhh. Yes. Especially there. Good guess."

"No guess. Experience." Fingers exploring. Entering. Feels good. I'm grooving on this. "Let me see clit please."

"Hell no."

"Show clit meat please."

"No. Watch where you're going, Red. Oh my god we're gonna die."

Swerve.

"That was close. Uhh. Uhh."

"Show please."

"Okay. But watch where you're going please. Uhh." Up goes my skirt. Down goes my thong.

"Oooh. Pretty. Foreplay now."

His freckled face dives past nipple this time, past tummy, and burrows deep in pursuit of clit meat.

I slam my thighs closed. "Lift your head up! Watch where you're going! I'm serious!"

"Foreplay now please."

"No. You're crazy. Safety first, remember?"

"Play with it."

"No."

"Play with it or foreplay now." Grinning. Grinning. Flicking very long tongue. "Make choice please."

He does have a very interesting tongue, but I choose the safe path. I begin to play with it. Red watches...my technique, I guess. How I rub it with two fingers. How I alternate between fold and flesh. Lubricating one with the wetness of the other. Check, check, he says, every now and then. Check. And steers somehow, without swerving.

Yeah. He'd better check-check it out. He'd better take notes to get it right when it's his turn. I'm thinking about his long tongue. Thinking about the long rest of him. Yeah.

I come, sweetly, my butt winding circles on the leather seat, and Red is grinning, grinning greedy, and saying: "More please."

I put up my hand. "No more. No more."

"Show."

"Show what? I showed you everything."

"No. Me show you," he says. "Wait please."

He slows the car and unzips himself. Red unzips a monster.

"You like?" he says, his head bopping to the bass.

"I like. It's very big." I reach for it, but he blocks my hand.

"Just wait till it gets hard please."

"You mean it's not hard?" I gasp.

Red is grinning. "Just making a joke," he assures. Grinning. Grinning. "Scared you, huh?"

Yeah.

# SEEING RED

It starts before we get into the apartment.

Going up the narrow stairwell, he unfastens my buttons and runs his hand inside, engaging silk with tenderness until he meets elastic and lifts the tight edge, touches his warm fingertips against waiting flesh, and says, "You know we're gonna do this. We're really gonna do this."

I'm on the rung above him, in the tight space. I pivot to face him. Steadying myself on his shoulders, swinging my calves in an upward movement, smoothly, one after the other, like a dance, I remove my shoes and panties and deposit them in his hand. "I hope you can handle it, Red."

He buries his head under my skirt between my thighs in the narrow stairwell. His exploration is catlike and hungry.

Here, pussy, pussy.

I close my eyes. Enjoy. We hear the sound of someone coming and drop my skirt back into place, skipping up the remaining stairs. Giggling.

Then we are at the door. My keys jangle on the ring. The surprising coolness of the air I had left on rushes past us out the open door. His hand is rubbing my midriff. My tongue is against his nipple. My toes stretch out to shove the door closed just as he is lifting me, carrying me, to my couch. We tear at each other's clothes. We are surrounded by the smell of roses. "The bedroom," I breathe. "The bedroom is in there." He's lifting me again, carrying me into the bedroom. Setting me down on the big bed Tyrone had loved. King size, for a king size lover, he had said. Tyrone was a king. Red is an emperor. He sets me down gently on the bed. I inhale. He pulls off what is left of his shirt and pants and steps back from the bed with one hand on his big penis. He is all length and leanness now. He is a lance at right angles to a lance. He comes back to the bed and climbs over me. Giving me his pussy, pussy lips to lick. I lick. I caress his long, smooth thighs. I caress his lance. "You like that. Wanna see it up close?" he says. "Show me," I say. He climbs up higher on my chest, resting it between my breasts. It is prettier up close. The darkest limb on his body. A slab of summer sausage. It rests so heavy on my tiddies, I am afraid of it. To make friends, I caress the velvety helmet of its head with my tongue. It is weeping salt. Red groans and slides his hips down my chest. "Wait a minute. Oh, baby, I gotta get up in you." He steps off and reaches down into the tangle of clothes and comes up with a condom in a plastic packet. He tears the packet with his teeth and stretches the condom down the penis and gets back over me with his hands on my thighs. I'm aware that I am being parted. "Oooh," I say, as it fills me. "You all right?" he says. "It's wonderful," I say. He leans down his face and we kiss. His hands hold my face, my neck. There is sweat. It is cold and we are perspiring. I am perspiring. He blesses my face, my neck, my ears with velvet lips. My tongue flickers over his cheeks. I am trying to taste the freckles on his face. They will taste like cinnamon, I know they will. There is movement in his hips. I kick up my legs as he pushes.

"Red—!" I pant. I shiver. "Red!"

# PACKING

We pack.

We make love.

We pack some more.

We run out of condoms.

We make love some more. Carefully.

The work gets done in half the time with Red making the trip to Joan's house to drop off my essentials while I ride to the storage warehouse with the movers. The last thing we pack is the thick Christmas comforter, which we spread on the floor for one more ferocious round of loving. Red hooks my ankles over his shoulder and pushes me around the floor until my flesh is awake with pleasure and my knees are too tingly for standing. Just when I think I can't take anymore, my confident red man flips me over and insinuates himself into a place back there that definitely did not beckon.

"Oh, shit, Red." I grab hold of the comforter, hollering.

I never liked this the few times me and Tyrone did it. It is dirty. It hurts too much. There is nothing in it for me but to wait it out. With Red, I am surprised to find myself coming. I'm hollering at this, then laughing. I push back against him hard, laughing with surprise at the pleasure. Red slaps my ass with an open hand and thrusts hard. Explodes in me. I shiver. I explode back. Laughing.

After that, he stretches out on his stomach and I get an idea. I come back in the room with a handful of rose petals and place each one lovingly on each freckle on his shoulder. He nods his head and calls me sweet. Silly. We are laughing at this. I begin to massage his speckled shoulders. He is still a mystery to me, this lover of Tawana and Joan. And now me. I am thoroughly loved. I say to him, "Truth please."

He rolls over, spilling the fragrant petals, pulls me atop him, kisses me. It is a good kiss, but I have a one track mind. "Truth," I repeat.

He chuckles. "Truth for truth."

"Deal."

"Ask the question," he says.

"You were crying yesterday."

"Hard one, Cindique. Real hard one."

"Truth for truth."

His face is serious. He mumbles, "Tawana and that guy…it doesn't look like she's ever coming back. I tried, but—."

"Impossible. You are the perfect lover. She is a fool."

"Thank you. I needed that."

I grab his big penis. "Can I steal you from her please? I hate her. The dumb bitch."

"You sure do speak your mind."

"It's the truth. She's an idiot. Don't think about her anymore. Think about me."

"Yeah," he says, softly. "She *is* my cousin after all."

# Rub It Please

I release him. Roll away from him. Wrap myself in the edge of the Christmas trees, reindeer, and five-point stars of the comfy comforter. The idea of incest…sometimes love is hard to find, I know, but there are enough good ones out there so you don't have to go marrying your brothers, sisters, cousins.

"Stop lying, Red."

Red frowns at the space I've put between us on the comforter, and turns his back to me. "Truth for truth," I hear him say. "I don't lie to you, you don't lie to me. This is hard enough to talk about. I'm ready to walk out of here right now."

"But, Red. I mean…damn. Your own cousin?"

His speckled shoulders tremble.

"Aw, Red. I don't mean it like that." A few minutes ago, I felt good with this man, and now his back is to me. He knocked the memory of Tyrone and his king-sized love right out of my head, and now his back is to me. I was thinking a few minutes ago that he just might be the one, and now—. I reach for his narrow little butt (it's got a rose petal on it) and give it a pinch. His shoulders shrink, but he doesn't make a sound.

"How close, Red?"

He doesn't turn to face me. "My grandmother is her grandmother's aunt. My mother is her grandmother's first cousin."

In my head, I reconstruct the family tree. "That makes her your fourth cousin, or third. It's hard to figure."

"Fourth."

"That's not so bad, I guess."

"Only when you think about it."

"I think it's illegal to marry a first cousin, right? And yucky to marry a second. But third and fourth…your son wasn't born with a tail or anything?"

He groans. I touch my fingertips to his back. I begin to draw circles on his back.

He says, "When I was living at home with my parents, before I moved out on my own, I was different from how I am now. I was saved and sanctified. I was born again."

"Red the master was a church boy?"

"Saved and sanctified."

"Red the butt master?" I whisper.

He shivers with his back still to me, and I can't tell if he's laughing or crying. He answers, "I was holy ghost baptized."

"Me, too. I was a Baptist."

"I was Oldtime Holiness. And a virgin."

I reach around and pet his flaccid manhood. "Not anymore, you're not."

"Six hours of service on Sunday. Bible study four nights a week. We weren't like some of these other churches they got around here today where you can do anything and be saved. We were serious about our churching. Our women didn't wear pants. Our men didn't drink or smoke. We didn't have any, not one single one, no teen mothers in our church."

"You guys were deep."

"Yeah. They felt my mom and dad were too liberal. Too loose. Because they let us watch TV and go to movies. Fire and brimstone, they warned."

"Real deep."

"Fire and brimstone. Maybe they were right," he says. "Tawana was coming to stay with us because she was having trouble at home. I heard my parents talk about this problem Tawana had, but they were never specific when we kids were around. The day came, and Cousin Tawana arrived from Mississippi. She was straight-up country. A hick. The way she talked, the way she dressed. It was bad. I didn't like her at all. She was okay looking, and she was my cousin, so I was totally not attracted to her. Plus she had that *problem* that my parents were whispering about. For some reason, however, she had her eyes on me, her little church boy cousin. She's two years older than me, you know?"

"Hmm. And how old are you?"

"Twenty-three."

"My ex is 23, too. He was the son of my favorite teacher. I've always liked older men."

"We got something in common, then."

"You like older men? Is that how you became the butt master?"

"Don't even try to be funny. If you didn't like it, you could've told me not to do it."

"I didn't say I didn't like it."

He doesn't answer.

"Damn. Stop being so sensitive, Red. If I didn't want you to do it, I would've stopped you. Just finish your story about how you fucked your own cousin."

Red groans.

"Red, you're gonna have to learn to chill. If you only know how much I'm digging you right now. I'm just playing with you. Finish the story."

He rolls over to face me again. I snuggle against his chest, and he wraps his arms around me.

"Well," he says, "I began to notice the strange side of Tawana after I had played a trick on her one night. She had done the cooking that day, so my mom and dad wanted me to tell her how good it tasted to lift her self-esteem, you know? My parents were big into that lifting your self-esteem stuff back then. Make a sinner feel good. Make her know you care about her and her soul. Anyway, I decided to kid her a bit. I told her the food was horrible. There wasn't enough salt, I complained. She just about freaked. She was crying and beating herself up and promising she would do better next time, and I'm trying to tell her that it was just a joke. I was just kidding. The food was fine. Just a joke. In our house we were holy, but we liked a good joke once in a while, I told her, and if you're gonna stay with us you gotta be able to take a joke. My parents told her, yes, yes, he was just joking. Praise the lord. She seemed to improve a little, though she went to bed early. The next day, everything seemed normal until out of the blue she asked me how her shoes looked. I looked down at them. They looked fine. Country, but fine. I told her so. Later she asked me about her dress. I told her it looked fine, and she seemed pleased. It went on like this for a few days, with her coming to me for approval of how she was dressed. If I ever hesitated telling her something she wore looked good, it came off immediately. If I showed I really liked something she had on, she became ecstatic."

I nod. "Aw, I know where sister girl was coming from. I've been there. She had Red on the brain. She had it bad. Your parents should've been paying attention. A girl like that'll do crazy shit."

"Tell me about it," Red says. "One day she wore a blue dress that I really did like, in a cousinly sort of way, and I told her so before she even asked me. It was like she had become queen of the world or something the way she went on. She went into her bedroom singing, I swear. When she came out, she sat down next to me, in that dress, and asked me if I would like to go to the movies with her. I said, sure. Why not? My parents thought it was a good idea, and they gave us money and told us to have a good time."

He is staring up at the ceiling, his hand tracing my thigh.

"Red, what happened?"

"Maybe if my parents had been more saved, more holy, they wouldn't have let us go. Fire and brimstone."

"Red?"

"We never made it to the movie theater," he says gloomily. "I was driving my father's car, and she told me she had to stop off at a friend's house first. I thought it was a funny kind of friend. She wasn't exactly sure where it was. She had the address written down on a sheet of paper. When she finally arrived at the house, there was a white man standing outside in the yard. She said, I think that's him. Then she got out of the car and followed the man inside the house. It was a small, ugly house way up there near Ft. Lauderdale. Real country-looking. Most of the yards were overgrown. There were rusted cars on most of the lawns. Just behind the last row of clapboard houses was the entrance to a trailer park that didn't look so affluent either. She was in there about an hour. When she came out and got back in the car, she seemed to be in outer space. She wasn't talking. She was hardly moving. Her eyes just seemed to stare off in the distance. I asked her, what's the matter? She burst out crying. Crying bad. I drove for a while, then pulled over and parked the car in the parking lot of a restaurant we were about to pass and put my arm around her. What's the matter, I said. You can talk to me. She said, that was my father. I said, what? I thought your father lived up in Mississippi. She said, that's not my father. That's my stepdad up in Mississippi. I said, your real dad is a white man? She said, yeah, and he told me not to come see him any more after this. She went back to boo-hooing, and I held her against my chest. Brushing her hair with my fingers. Trying to soothe her. She was sniffling against my neck, saying something I couldn't make out. I said, what? She said, I'm glad you're here with me. I'm glad I came down here and met you. I said, yeah, me too. Brushing her hair with my fingers. She said something else. I said, what? She said, I'm glad you're my cousin. You're good Christian people, like my mama. You care about people. Boo-hoo. You make cruel jokes, but you're nice inside. I said, yeah. I'm sorry about the joke. Don't cry, Tawana. I should never have made that joke. I was just joking, you know? I know now, she said, because I know that you like me. The way you're holding me, this is good. This'll help me forget all about my problem with fathers. She snuggled into me tighter. She was wearing a perfume that made me think of flowers and a cool breeze blowing. She rested her face against my neck and her hand fell into my lap. It was mostly on my thigh. I remember that I was wearing jeans. I remember I was fighting against a shameful erection for my boo-hooing cousin whose cooking I had picked at. Her face was against my neck, her lips when she moved them, caressed the underside of my chin like butterfly wings. The way I was holding her, even though she was my cousin, was like what I had seen the cool boys at school doing with their girlfriends. It felt good. I understood now why they did it. It felt good to just hold somebody like that. I had never had a girlfriend, you know? I had never held anyone. Her hand in my lap squeezed my thigh, and she mumbled something else I couldn't make out. I said, what? She said, my chest hurts so much. So much, cousin. Boo-hoo. My chest. I'm sorry about that, I said. My boyfriend back home used to help me when I got sad and my chest hurt like this, she said. What did your boyfriend back home do when your chest hurt, I asked her. He would rub it, she said. Rub it, I asked. Yes, she said. He would rub it up at the top. Give me your hand. She took my hand, and that felt good too, just her taking my hand, and she placed the fingers at the base of her throat, just inside her collar. I began to rub her chest with my fingers. Not a real hard rubbing, a light rubbing, because my fingers were trembling, trying to rub without touching the top of the breasts. She said, that feels good, real good, but it's not stopping the pain. Boo-hoo. I'm in such pain, cousin. I said, what can I do? She said, go lower, okay? Like that, I asked. (Going lower inside her collar, staying to the middle, between her breasts, touching them, but trying not to touch them anymore than was necessary to rub her, and it was warm and wet in there, felt like tiny hairs or something were standing up on her skin. I found myself in pain, too, and it took me a few seconds to figure what it was. My penis was alive in my pants, and the way I was sitting, it had nowhere to grow.) Yes, she said, like that. Oh but it still hurts. Oh I wish you weren't my cousin. Oh I wish you were my boyfriend so that you could do it right. But you are my cousin and you can't help me because you can't be objective about it. Oh I'm in such pain. I said, I can be objective, I can. She said, you won't embarrass me or make cruel jokes, will you? No, I said. I will not embarrass you or make cruel jokes. I just want to help you. Oh, she said, I'm in such pain. Boo-hoo. Such pain. Here is what you have to do, Cousin Roderick, you have to go lower, okay? You have to open the clasp of the brassiere so that you can go lower. Please don't make cruel jokes when you open it. Please don't embarrass me. I'm already in such pain. You think you can do that? Open the clasp? I said, I think I can, I think so, thinking about hell and fire and brimstone. She said, you must be sure, Cousin Roderick. Boo-hoo. Here's what you have to do, okay? You must turn your head, look out the window, as you open the clasp. Please do not embarrass me. I'm in such pain. Okay, I said. I can do it. Okay, she said. Go ahead and open the clasp, but look away, look away, Cousin Roderick. So my trembling hand reached inside her dress and opened the clasp while I stared out the window at a giant green trash dumpster. With the clasp out of the way, I was now able to press my fingers down the center of her chest, without touching her breasts too much. (Her breasts are heavy, but they are separated by a perfect cleft down the middle. But I did not see this, I only felt it—the fine hairs, the warmth, the dampness of skin on either side of my two fingers, the sprig of nipple set on a high ridge that sponged against my wrist as I made the chaste up and down movements on the chest of my cousin—I saw none of this because I was looking out the window at the unmoving dumpster.) Oh, she said, oh, that feels real good. Real good. That's just what I need. That's just the way my boyfriend does it. You're not looking are you? No, I said. Good, she said, then I'm going to unbutton the dress so that your hand doesn't pop the buttons. I felt the movement of fabric and limbs as she unbuttoned her dress. There, she said, that's much better. Yes, oh yes. Boo-hoo. Keep doing it. Boo-hoo. Do it like my boyfriend back in Mississippi. He is so good at this. Oh how I miss him. Oh how I would kiss him and hug him for doing this for me. You're doing a good job, too, cousin, but I can't kiss you because you are my cousin. Oh I wish I could kiss you all over your face and mouth and throat and chest. I wish I could rub your chest. I wish I could rub inside your pants like I do for my boyfriend. I wish I could sit on your lap with my panties off like I do for him. He likes it. He likes it a lot, and you rub my chest just as good as him. It's not fair. Have you ever seen a girl with her shirt off? Boo-hoo. Have you ever seen a girl with her panties off? Boo-hoo. My boyfriend back in Mississippi has seen it lots of times. I'm always taking my panties off to show him. It's just not fair because you rub my chest just as good as him and you'll never see me with my panties off. Oh I wish we weren't cousins. I would sit on your lap with my panties off and kiss your face and your chest because you make my chest feel so good. Oh that feels good. And you're not embarrassing me at all. You're not being cruel. You're really such a good cousin. Keep rubbing it. Oh. Then, suddenly, she quieted. What, I said. What? The pain, she said, has moved inside the breast. Do you think you can rub the left breast without embarrassing me? Tawana, I said, I can't. I just can't. I'm dying here. I'm bursting. I can't rub your breast without embarrassing you. If I rubbed it, I would embarrass you, I would embarrass you like crazy. She said, even though you're a Christian? I said, yes. She said, even though I'm your cousin? I said, yes, boo-hoo. Boo-hoo. She sat up and kissed me on the throat. I was still looking at the dumpster. Turn your face and look at me, she said. I turned my face. The sweat had soaked my forehead. The tears had fogged my eyes. I tried not to look down at her bare breasts. They were golden globes of—. She kissed me on the mouth and held me in her arms. She found my hands and put them one after the other behind her back so that I was holding her, too. We kissed like that for a long time, and I wasn't thinking at all about fire and brimstone or the fact that my grandmother was her grandmother's aunt. Then she leaned back so that I could see her beautiful chest. They were beautiful. They were golden globes of—grace and glory, hallelujah! She hoisted up her dress, and took off her panties, exposing a triangle of fur and lips. See, she said, see what a girl looks like with her panties off? Tell me how it looks to you, and don't make cruel jokes about it, okay? It looks beautiful, I said, glory. Do you like it a lot, she asked. Yes, I like it a whole lot, I answered, glory. Then she took my hand and placed it between her legs where it was slippery and sweet smelling. Rub it, she said, like you rubbed my chest, and she leaned forward and put her mouth on mine again. You're such a good kisser, she said. Oh, that feels so good the way you're rubbing it. The way you're playing with it. So much better than my boyfriend. He doesn't play with it nearly as good as you. I hate him. I'm gonna dump him. Are you my new boyfriend or my cousin? Your new boyfriend, I answered. She said, then we're gonna have to go in the back seat so I can sit on your lap with my panties off. We can't do it in the front. The steering wheel always gets in the way."

# CAN I KEEP YOU?

"And?"

"And we went in the backseat. And it changed my life. For the next couple weeks, we broke all the rules of my saved and sanctified home, sneaking around to screw. She got pregnant like a month after we started. I was 17, she was 19. My mother cried as much as my father at the wedding."

"Your parents are crazy letting you marry a girl like that. Damn."

"She was pregnant."

"So? Girls get pregnant all the time. It don't mean nothing. Boo-hoo."

"You gotta have morals and values, Cindique. That's what's wrong with people today."

"That's what's wrong with you *church folk*. You gotta learn to live in the real world. That's crazy what they let you do. Y'all were just kids. Boo-hoo. Boo-hoo."

"Stop picking at me. Look who's talking. You got married young, too."

"That's different. I was in love."

"Me, too," he says. "At the wedding, I learned the *secret* of Cousin Tawana from Mississippi. I overheard two aunts talking about it. She had to leave her house because they found out that her stepdad had been abusing her from the time she was young. If I didn't love her before, I began to love her then. I was a Christian. I was brought up to have pity on people. Her little problem made me pity her."

"You loved her?"

"*Love* her," corrects the man who had set my knees to tingling. "Yeah. I love her very much."

"Boo-hoo."

"You got that right."

"Boo-hoo. Boo-hoo." I poke my tongue out at him, but it's all I can do to keep it light. I'm seriously jealous. "What does she look like?"

"Real pretty. Fine. Sexy. Big legs. Booty to burn—." He's taking too much pleasure in describing her, smiling all wide, sighing up at the ceiling in awe. "—lighter than you. Even lighter than me. But that booty—."

"Shut up. I don't want to hear anymore of that. A girl with lighter skin than me, and a bigger booty, too? Naw, naw, naw. What about her new boyfriend?"

"Some old pops. About forty, fifty. Big stomach. Bald head."

"What! She's stupid. That's her bust. You're a keeper. The way you look, the way you rock it, I would sit on your lap with my panties off all day. Boo-hoo. Boo-hoo. Shit." I'm feeling reckless. I cross my fingers. I may not be as pretty as Tawana...I look into his eyes. "Can I keep you?"

He starts to nibbling on my lips. It's a good kiss, as they all have been, but it doesn't feel like a *yes*. It feels a little bit like a brush off. Okay, so he needs time to get over Cousin Tawana. Okay, so this is just a fuck thing we're doing. Okay, so why does it feel so right? Some part of him is resisting as I hold him, pulling away, going back to the backseat of his father's car, and I lock my arms around him. "Crazy Tawana," I laugh. "Why would she want some old man anyway?"

"How would I know? His money, I guess. He's got money." He pushes me off and goes for the cigarettes in my bag on the floor in the corner. He scoops up the pack and pats one out, slips it in his mouth, and lights up with my keychain lighter. Now he stands naked at the window, with his hands atop his head, smoking. It's a real nice view. He has the body of a long distance runner. Faultless shoulders, arms like strong rope, a perfectly flat stomach. The lean, strong legs. In the rays of the dying sun, his color looks like highly polished bronze. After a while, he groans and says, "We better get going."

"Truth for truth."

"I told you the truth."

"About Groan?"

He turns from the window. "What about her?"

"What's up with that? If you love Tawana so much...what's that all about?"

Squinting from the sun, he pulls the cigarette from his mouth and styles it between two fingers like a joint. "What's *what* all about?"

"You and Groan—."

He puts up a hand to shade his face from the sun. "What about me and Joan?"

"I saw you *together*."

The naked man moves from the window into a shaded part of the room. Laughing. Shoves the cigarette between his lips to stop from laughing. Puts a hand up to hold onto the wall to stop from falling from the laughing. I'm so funny. I'm so ridiculous to suggest a thing like that. "You ain't see nothing going on between me and Joan. You a trip. Ha-ha. Joan's my boss. Joan's my friend. You ain't see nothing. Ha-ha." His long rope of dick flapping against his thigh.

"I know what I saw. I saw you kiss her."

"I did not kiss her. You're crazy, Cindique. You didn't see nothin. Ha-ha."

"I figured you all wanted me to catch you, as bold as you were."

"It's just not true. Me and that old woman. Ha-ha."

"Truth for truth, Red. You're a lying ass mofo."

He flicks the cigarette down to the hardwood floor and mashes it out with his bare foot. He comes over to where I'm lying with the comforter bunched up against my stomach like a pillow and shakes a finger in my face. "Truth for truth, you're the liar. Don't be calling me no liar. Don't be making up stuff about me. Don't be making me mad. Talking about my friend like that. Shame on you. And you're gonna be staying in her house." He's standing in fragrant rose petals like sandals. His rope of dick flapping against his leg. Shaking that finger in my face. "—making trouble for people who help you out. No good deed goes unpunished. Shame on you."

I'm beginning to see what's really going on, and I'm sorta cool with it. Adultery. Christian guilt. It's the kind of things consenting adults do. Red doesn't have to worry. Nobody's gonna get hurt because of me. Glory hallelujah! But here in this room, just between the two of us after a day of loving like this, truth for truth *is* truth for truth. "—Red, if you're trying to protect her, don't worry, I won't tell nobody. That's not why I brought it up—."

He jumps in my face, cutting me off.

"Just get your clothes on, and pack up the rest of this shit!" he says. "—With your black ass."

# PART III

▼

# It Was All Bullshit

We drive without speaking until the sun sets, leaving behind this beautiful layer of colors on the horizon. It is so beautiful, so beautiful, and I am still stinging. Bounce, bounce, bounce, and then the beauty is gone and it is dark. It is black. Black. Black. Black. Bounce. There is no music in the car, no sound, nothing, except the roar of the Bronco's engine, the ping and ping of its tires spitting small stones out of its way. Red is seriously speeding.

I say to him, "There's a hotel coming up. Just drop me off there. I can take care of myself. Tell Joan I said thanks, but I don't need anybody's help. I'll pass by and get my car from work tomorrow. I'll take a cab or something."

"Why?" The first word he's said since we got into the car. He eases up off the gas, and the car slows to a moderate clip. He tries to sound reasonable, even friendly. "But your stuff's already at the house. She already prepared the guest house for you and everything. Don't take it out on her because you're mad at me. You don't have any clean clothes with you."

"I'll be fine, *mom*. Just stop the damned car, okay? Shit."

He stops the car on the side of the road across the street from the hotel. I ain't too cute, or too black, to walk across the street. I push open the door and swing my legs out. When he grabs my hand, I swear to god, I'm about ready to snatch my scissors out the bag and stick him. *Lying ass born again hypocrite punk.* I spin to face him. "Whachu want from me, Roderick Redd?"

He plays his cocky smirk, but it's so transparent, and he squeezes my hand, as though the touch of him is the answer to everything, and he says, "Truth for truth."

I want to slap him. "You got to be out of your damned mind. I ain't playin no games with you. I hate your punk ass."

He does not give up. He tries to persuade with his eyes. The twinkle in them. I frown it away, but his persistence melts the hardness. Then he flips on the playful voice that had turned me on earlier: "Truth for truth please."

"Oh what the hell," I say, pulling out of his grasp. Softening, because of his eyes. I love the way he looks at me. I love the way I feel when he looks at me. But I still hate him, and I want him to know it. "Meet me 'cross the street at the hotel. And hurry up, so I can be done with your ass."

"Okay," says Mr. Cheerful.

I pass in front of the Bronco, holding up my hand to stop traffic as I cross the busy road. Swinging my hips. Showing him my *black ass* in motion. The wind, which has picked up, is lashing the tail of my skirt. He's right—I do not have a change of clothes. Everything's at Joan's house already. I go to the hotel's parking lot and watch as he U-turns onto the property, parks the Bronco, and steps out. There is the chirp-chirp of his alarm being automatically set as he strides across the lot in an over-sized royal blue and amber FUBU shirt and relaxed-fit jeans hanging low on his hips. He is tall. Six-two. Six-three. With a sexy walk.

2 Cool 4 U.

Yeah.

I'm real soft now, but I still hate him, and I want him to know.

There's a bench in front of a row of newspaper machines off to the side of the hotel's entrance. He goes there and steps up on the seat and balances his butt on the high back of the bench with his feet on the seat. My mama would have killed him. She hates when people sit on the arms of chairs or on the backs of chairs. Sit on the damned seat, that's what it's there for. He is posing. His long legs are casually open, leaving space for me to sit between them all comfy, if I so choose. *With my black ass.* I amble over and climb right up on the back of the bench next to him. He folds his arms across his chest and fixes his gaze on me. "Truth?"

"Truth for truth."

"Your virginity."

"Oh, this is so wack. Where did this come from?"

"Truth for truth."

"But that's a hard one."

"No backing out. Play the game fair." Nodding his shaved head. Smiling. Showing all his straight, beautiful teeth.

"I'm not backing out," I say, notching my toes in the grooves of the seat for a more secure balance on the back of the bench. My legs aren't as long as his. I can't lean forward and rest my elbows on my knees without tipping over, the way he does, looking all cool. With my toes fixed in the grooves, I am free to move my hands a little bit. "My virginity is kinda complicated, Roderick Redd."

Head all tilted to the side. "Naw. You're talking crazy, Cindique. Virginity is virginity. You can only lose it once. That's the gospel truth. Now fess up, and gimme a smoke."

I stand up on the seat and reach into my bag. He eyes me from top to bottom. He mouths, "It do look good." He can look all he wants. He's never touching this *black ass* again. I pass him a cigarette and my lighter. He forms a cup over his mouth with his hand, lights up, and begins to smoke, handing back the lighter between crossed fingers all cool.

I sigh in resignation and begin to explain to him, "I was 15. I had two men who loved me," as I re-mount my perch, my toes digging into the grooves of the seat. Hands again gripping the hard rail of wood that my big *black ass* is balanced on. "One of them, I hadn't met yet. One of them, I was gonna marry. We were so in love. He was attentive to my needs. What needs did I have at 15? He was older. He was cute. He listened to me, that was enough. I liked him because I liked my teacher, and she was his mom. He knew I hated living at home with mama who was a slave driver. She didn't even want to hear that I was doing good in school. All she wanted was for me to take care of my little sisters, four of them, while she did double shifts at the hospital. Coming home complaining about the house not being clean. I had to study. I had homework to do, I would say. I was an honors student. I had straight A's until I dropped out of school. But what about me, she would say. You think I like working these hours? If your daddy would pay his child support, things would be better for us. She used to slap me, too, if I got fresh. Mama was fast with her hands. Lordy, lordy, Mama knew how to slap. If I never see that crazy bitch again…well, me and Tyrone were gonna run away from home. He was gonna rob a liquor store in the neighborhood that didn't have security. That was the plan. He was always a man with a plan. We were gonna run away to Vegas with my fake ID and find a preacher. I would've let him take my virginity without getting married, but he wanted to do right by me because he loved me and that's the way the Bible said you were supposed to do it. So we would kiss and feel each other up. He was real good at that kind of heat. It would get me so hot, I would go home and spend hours in the shower or under the sheets, kinda in half sleep, kinda grooving, and not do mama's work. And that would get me in more trouble with mama…with her *black ass.*"

I glance up at Red. He flinches. Yeah. There's a small, little frown beginning at the bottom of his face. There's sadness and apology in his eyes. He puts the cigarette in his mouth and hides his face behind a puff of smoke. Yeah. Keep frowning, little red bone. I can cut, too.

I say to him, "You know when my man ran out on me and I was scared, I asked mama if my little sister could come stay with me for a while, and she told me, come home, your room is still waiting for you, and the housework you left unfinished, too. You think I forgot about your work? It's right here waiting for you. I'll be damned if you set foot in this house without doing it. She's crazy, I tell you. Anyway, I couldn't wait to get to Vegas. Fuck mama. Fuck school. I wanted to fuck. Let me get a hit of that, Roderick Redd."

He holds the cigarette up to my mouth and, cautiously, puts his hand on the back of my neck as I take a few hits, exhale, throw my head back. Look up at the black sky. Look up at the twinkling stars, under which Tyrone and I had hatched our plans and dreamed.

"It was all bullshit. That liquor store had security out the ass. I took Tyrone there and showed him the two police cruisers parked across the street. He didn't even want to hear about it. He accused me of trying to back out on him. He told me he loved me, and he wanted to hear me say I loved him back. I said I did, and he said, so then don't go messing up the plan. Stay with the man who has a plan. He showed me the gun he had got that day from his cousin. He had it stuck in his waistband gangster style. He took it out and made me hold it, right there with the police cruisers across the street from the liquor store. I told him I was scared. I told him take it back, I don't like guns. He took it back, laughing. It ain't even loaded, he told me. Think I would do a robbery with a loaded gun? They give you extra time in jail if the gun is loaded. I'm not that stupid, he assured me."

Roderick Redd is looking at me with his mouth open. Incredulous. I reach up and flick the long tail of ash hanging off the cigarette balanced on his lip. He says, "And you married this guy? He wasn't too bright."

I respond in my best Forrest Gump: "He wasn't my kinfolk neither, Cousin Roderick."

Red averts his eyes.

The rail of wood is seriously hurting my butt, so I hop down, and lean against it instead.

"That was like a Wednesday night. The big liquor store robbery was set for Saturday night, at five minutes to eleven, just before they closed. The other guy who took my virginity, I met him the next day. I had read an ad in the paper about some quick money I could make, $500, for two hours work. Modeling. They were looking for a variety of female types. You had to be attractive. You had to be 18. You had to have two pieces of ID. Well, I was attractive, I was female, I was variety. So I went and bought another fake ID, a library card. I already had a fake driver's license that I used for cigarettes and wine coolers. The studio was at this warehouse down by the docks. A half dozen other girls were already there. Leggy blondes. Brunettes with painted faces and big breasts. A redhead who was clearly high on something. A variety of female types. White girls. It was a tryout for a small part in a movie. There was a door they went through one at a time. About a half hour or so later, they would return and go to a caged window where a fat man with a bushy moustache and a grimy shirt peeled off hundreds from a stack of bills to pay them. All of the girls came back through the door looking beaten up and disheveled. One girl, the redhead, came back with her blouse open and her saggy looking breasts drooping down to her navel. They were very ugly breasts. There were scars on them, and what looked like burn marks, all across her chest and her overhanging stomach. She went to the barred cage just like that and collected her money. She was so high it made no difference to her that her blouse was open. Luckily, one of the other girls got up and fastened it for her before letting her out the main door. When I saw that, I began to worry about what kind of movie it was. I asked the girl who had helped the redhead. She looked at me and said: Porno. I started thinking, naw, naw, naw. The girl said to me, your first time, huh? If you want, we can go in together. It's easier doing it with a girl the first time. Guys are too rough, the girl said to me. She leered at me with her hand all in my lap."

I can see Red is really getting into my story. He's really digging this part. He nods his head and asks, "Did you go in with her?"

"No!" I say. "Hell no."

"But you did go in?"

"It was $500. The money was real. It was enough to get us to Vegas, get us married, get us started in our new perfect life away from my tyrant mother and Tyrone's repeated failures in the educational system. Really, it was a lot of money. More than Tyrone could make trying to rob that liquor store without bullets. I didn't want him to get killed. Plus—."

Nodding. Completing my sentence for me. "Plus you wanted to get fucked."

"I wanted to see what it was like. No one would ever find out."

He snorts. "But you're wrong. Every one would find out. It's porno. You're making a movie. People would be watching you all over the world."

Yeah, I see where he's coming from. *Now.* But I didn't think about it like that back then on that day in the warehouse by the docks. The place was kind of out of the way and dimly lit. The action was taking place in a back room, where no one could see it. It looked like a secret. No, it had not occurred to me that what we were doing in that secret location would eventually be watched in thousands of homes.

"Anyway," I say, "I did go in. I was like the last one to go. There was a bed with curtains behind it and a bureau beside it to make it look like a bedroom. There was a video camera set up on a tripod. There was the guy I was telling you about, Jake, behind it. He was about thirty. Medium tall. Ebony skin. Handsome face. A sweet face. Smiled a lot. Big, pretty, white teeth. He was totally naked. His dick was long like, damn—like yours. I sat down on the bed, and he turned off the video camera. I was like, what's going on? What are you doing? Aren't we making the porno? He was like, how old are you? Twenty, I said. He said, what year were you born? I told him the fake year I had memorized. He said, what month? I told him. He said, what high school do you go to? I told him. He said, I thought you said you were twenty? Oops. I said, I'm sorry, sir, I thought you said what high school *did* I graduate from? He was like, have a nice day, young lady. I was like, but I'm really twenty, I have ID. He was like, take a hike, kid, before you get hurt. You're cute and all, but if I film you, I'll go to jail. I don't need that kinda heat. He started to put on his clothes. I pleaded with him. He was like, naw, naw, naw. I was like, if we do it with the camera off, would you still give me the money? He was like, aw, hell no. That's prostitution. That's even worse. Are you a cop or something? Are you working for the cops? No, but I need that $500, I told him. Why do you need so much money, he asked. So that my boyfriend won't have to rob a liquor store for us to get married, I explained. He said, straight up? I said, yes. And he burst out laughing. He said, you know what? You're too funny. You made my day. I'm gonna give you the money. Hell, it's only money. I got lots of money. Wait here. Then he went into a back room and came out with $500 and gave it to me. Now beat it, he said, and good luck on your little marriage. I was so happy that I reached up and gave him a kiss on the cheek. Thank you, thank you, thank you, sir. Jake, he said. Thank you, Jake, I said. He added, and don't be hanging around porno studios anymore. You're too good for this. Too cute. I left for the door, and he said, you know that kiss you gave me was the first kiss I had all day, and I've been fucking all day. Well, I said, that's because you made me happy by doing this wonderful thing, Jake. He was like, how old are you really, Muffin Domingo? I said, Muffin is not my real name. My real name is Cindique Sanders, and I'm 18. He said, that's a beautiful name. Cindique. How old are you really, Cindique? I said, 16. He said, how old are you really, Cindique? I said, 15. He said, damn. I thought so. You look about the age of my little sister. She's in ninth grade. Me too, I said. He said, damn. What the hell are you doing getting married at 15, Cindique? You know, I feel I would be doing you a favor if I took that money back and did a porno with you instead. I got all sassy with him: That's what I came here for! I ain't scared of sex. When my boyfriend and me get married this weekend, I'm gonna have all the sex I want. He said, are you a virgin, Cindique? I said, no. He said, yes you are. I said, no I'm not. He said, why hasn't your boyfriend had sex with you? I said, because he's a Christian. He said, a Christian who's gonna rob a liquor store? Not anymore, I said, holding up the money. He said, but have you done *anything* with him? We've done lots, I said, and I told him about how Tyrone had sucked my tiddies and fingered me and how I had played with his dick so hard one night that white stuff had gushed out. I was proud of my limited sexual experience. Jake got serious and said, you know what, Cindique? I'm gonna ask you to do something that could get me into a lot of trouble, but I feel I have to do it. So you're gonna have to sign a paper for me before I do it, okay? I said, what are you gonna ask me to do? He said, give me a second, let me write it down. He went to a drawer and pulled out a steno pad and wrote something on it. He passed it to me. It read, *I Cindique Sanders am consenting to have Jacob Showalter eat my pussy.* And he had drawn a line under it for me to sign my name. My heart beat faster in my chest after reading that. Won't that be illegal, I asked him. Not if you sign it, he said. Why do you want to eat me, I said. Because, he said, you are so clean. So fresh. I was like, but what do you get out of it? He said, when you have great feelings for someone, you get pleasure out of pleasuring them. Please let me eat your pussy, Cindique. Let me eat it now while it is clean and fresh and sweet and pure. Let me eat you now while just looking at you makes my mouth water to touch you, to see you laugh, to see you come. So I took off my pants and let him eat me. It was really good. Better than all of the showers I had had. Better than all of the nights rubbing myself under the sheets. Better than Tyrone's hand under my dress on his mom's porch late at night. Jake took his time. Licked everything. Even my booty. Tears were like pouring out of my eyes. My breath was coming in short. Ohh. His tongue was doing tricks. Playing me like an instrument. Tap, tap, tap. Then it was scooping me out like I was a bowl that had ice cream in it. He made me cry out. He made me meow. I was like meditating. I was like on another plane. I was like in a trance, a dream like place, where I was just this good feeling coming from my coochie. I had no idea of time. Just coochie pleasure. Somehow my shirt had come off and my breasts were exposed. My eyes were closed, and I felt his hands on my nipples, then his mouth. I opened my eyes. He said, I'm sorry. I'm not supposed to be sucking these, but they're so big for such a young girl. Those nipples! I told him, go ahead, finish sucking them. He was like, well, you're gonna have to sign for it. He got up and tore off another sheet of steno and wrote. *I Cindique Sanders am consenting to have Jacob Showalter fondle and kiss my breasts.* I quickly signed on the line he had drawn, and he got back to sucking my breasts and I went back to my trance of pleasure. We were naked on the bed like that, with him kissing my breasts and his fingers in my coochie, and I pulled his face up, and we sucked on each other's tongues. I could feel his penis making friction against the mouth of my slit, as we sucked tongues and grooved on the good feeling. I said to him, I'm ready. He said, ready for what? I said, I'm ready to sign for you to stick it in my coochie. He was like, there is no such contract. I was like, please, please, please, Mr. Jake. I want to do it with you. He said, no, this business is too dangerous, and I began to cry, and he said, don't cry, don't cry, don't cry, as he rocked his body atop mine in a pleasing rhythm. I lifted my legs and wrapped them around his back. I wanted it to be complete, but he wouldn't let me. As he rocked, I rubbed my coochie against his big wonderful thing which he would never allow to go in me. I tried to slip it in, but he wouldn't let me. I kept rubbing, and I came hard. Crying. After that, he took me in the back and we showered together. He lathered me, kissed me, held me. He worshipped my body, and he never asked me to do anything for him. He said that being with me was enough. I wanted to worship his delicious black body, to lick him, to suck him, mmm, oh he looked so tasty, but he wouldn't let me. When I got out, he had a still camera and he said, I want to take one picture to remember you by. Just one. I went to the bed and posed for him. He snapped the picture. One picture. Then he came to the bed and he held me. He said, I have another idea. You're not going to elope until Saturday night, right? Can I be your boyfriend until you elope? I know it sounds crazy, but you make me young again. You bring back the childhood I never had because I got into this damned business too young. I've been fucking women, and men too, since I was thirteen. It's my dick. My big, black dick. Everybody wants to be penetrated by it. But you, you, you, you wonderful thing, you brought back my innocence. I want to be your ninth grade boyfriend for as long as we have left. Please let me see you again. Tomorrow? I'll pick you up. We'll go somewhere. I'll take you on a trip. We can go on my boat. I want to do something good for you because you did this good thing or me. Of course, I said yes. When he picked me up the next day, he had a copy of the Polaroid he had taken of me. It was beautiful. He gave it to me, but I gave it back because I was scared Tyrone might accidentally find it. He put it back in the envelope with the two handwritten contracts I had signed. I will cherish these forever, he said."

"And what happened?"

"I skipped school and went to the Bahamas with him on his boat. We fished and made out and took pictures, and he touched me with his tongue all day and nothing else. He took my virginity with his tongue. Of course, I fell in love with him. Saturday morning, he called and broke up with me. I cried all day. Saturday night, I showed Tyrone the money. Told him it was my life savings. He said, good, now I don't have to rob that liquor store for you. Then we got on a Greyhound bus to Vegas. That's where we got married and Tyrone took my virginity with his penis. It hurt a whole lot the first couple times, but then felt better."

# WHERE YOU GO, I'LL GO ALSO

Roderick Redd hops down from the back of the bench and takes my hand. Raises it to his lips. Kisses it. "Don't go in that hotel, Cindique. Or don't go in there alone. I like you. I really like you. I mean, uhm, you're not like any girl I've ever met before. Back at your old place, uhm, I don't know what got into my head. My life is so screwed. I was thinking about Tawana and how my birthday just passed, and we were supposed to get together, but she decided to go out with the old pops instead, and brought the boy over so that I could babysit him while she went out to have a good time with this guy on my birthday. It hurt, it hurt. She came by that night, when they had finished, to pick up the boy. She said she had a birthday gift for me, and the way she said it, I thought, oh, she's coming back to me. But it was a cheap watch like the kind you buy in a drugstore for three or four dollars as an afterthought, and I knew that's what it was. An afterthought, while she and the old pops stopped in the drugstore to buy condoms and cigarettes. An afterthought, after all the years we were together. An afterthought, after it was her who had pursued me, and not the other way around. It hurt. It hurt. I wasn't seeing straight. I wasn't thinking straight when I yelled at you. Don't go into that hotel. Don't go in there alone, Cindique."

He gets down on his knees. It feels kinda like a marriage proposal. And he says, "Wherever you go tonight, I'll go with you."

I say, "Even if I sleep at Joan's? If I sleep at Joan's tonight, will you be there with me?"

He lowers his head and lets go of my hand. The wedding is off.

(Boo-hoo.)

"Good night, Red. It was fun. Call me when you can deal with the truth. Your wife is a bitch and she's gone."

He's still on his knees.

"Have a nice life, church boy." I shrug and go into the lobby of the hotel. It doesn't look too cheap. The carpet on the floor is freshly vacuumed, and it doesn't stink. The banner advertises *78.99 A Night King Sized Bed Free Breakfast From 7:00 A.M. to 9:00.* A bit high for the room, but the free breakfast is a good deal. Then again, I'll be lucky if I have an appetite tomorrow after the crap with Red today. I look back outside. He's still on his knees out there.

It's too much. I move away from the entrance. It's too much to take. A grown man acting like that. Embarrassing. To get my mind off him, I explore the lobby. I'm in luck. Around by the bathrooms, I discover a gift shop that sells T-shirts, short sets, bathing suits, and robes with the hotel's logo on them. So I pay for the room with my credit card. Then I go back to the gift shop and buy a couple T-shirts and shorts to sleep in tonight and as a change of clothes for tomorrow. It's not top quality stuff, so it takes me about a half hour to find something passable. Then I am finished, ready to go up to my room, take a shower, and get freshened up. As I pass through the lobby, I sneak a peek back outside, and he is gone. Thank god. If he had still been out there, I don't know what I might have done. I might have softened. I might have stayed hard.

They put me on the sixth floor. I ride the elevator up. My room is number 623. The elevator door opens and I look down the hall to where I imagine 623 will be and I see Tyrone.

He has his back to me. He is talking to a hotel security guard, who glances over and gives me a friendly finger wave. Tyrone turns.

His grin.

I duck back into the elevator, push the button quick, quick, quick, ride it down to the first floor, run through the lobby, and burst out the front door into the parking lot.

Red's Bronco is already gone.

# PART IV

# WHO IS MR. WONDERFUL?

I have always loved love.

I married real young and real bad the first time, but it didn't change my mind. I still loved love. No matter how bad it got between me and Tyrone, I continued to dream of Prince Charming and his beautiful princess living happily ever after in a castle filled with gold. I never found this notion to be silly. Why shouldn't there be a princess in peril? Why shouldn't there be a prince who rescues? Why shouldn't they live happily ever after? What's wrong with a castle and lots and lots of gold? There I was with my black eye and my notepad (and Tyrone out with some woman) and I'm trying to write the truest story of true love that ever happened. Actually, I began the story as an assignment when I was in Mrs. Lassiter's Honors English class, but I needed some life experience with Tyrone before I was able to complete it. Marriage to a fool will give you all the experience you will ever need.

I called it *Summer Rose*.

Once upon a time, there was a stripper named Summer Rose, who worked at a club in the worst part of town because she was under age and only the shadiest clubs would let her dance there. Summer Rose was a beautiful girl with smoky skin and dark hair and eyes. No one knew whether she was black or Puerto Rican or Indian because of the way she looked. She was the favorite at the club, and all of the customers, both men and women, used to give her twice the amount of tips they gave the other girls. This did not make Summer Rose popular with the other dancers, who plotted against her and decided to jump her in the parking lot after her shift. They would disfigure her so that no one would pay to see her dance anymore. They were serious. They had done it before to other dancers they had been jealous of.

On the night when the other dancers were set to beat up Summer Rose after her shift, a well-dressed man walked over and sat down at the table upon which she was dancing. She could not see his face too well because of the wide-brimmed felt hat that he was wearing. She became very interested in him because he was tipping hundred-dollar bills. Now, Summer Rose in the three weeks that she had danced at the club had received hundred-dollar tips quite a few times from the patrons, for she was the most alluring dancer there, but nothing like this. The well-dressed man gave her hundred after hundred for her dances. At the end of her three-song set, she had exactly one thousand dollars in her garter.

When the well-dressed man asked her to dance for him privately in the VIP room, Summer Rose agreed. It was understood that dancers in the VIP room received no less than a hundred dollars for the "special" dances they performed for their patrons. State law forbid touching of any sort in strip clubs, but it was understood by all the dancers that a patron who paid the hundred-dollar VIP tip, and was concealed from public view by the fogged glass and the dimmed lights of that private chamber, would be allowed some license to tactile inquisitiveness. The well dressed man kept Summer Rose in the VIP room all night long, decorating her garter with hundred dollar bills like they were going out of style. He did not touch her once, except incidentally to put another hundred-dollar bill in her garter when she had performed a particularly pleasing turn during her dance. At the end of the night, just before the club closed at sunrise, the man got up to leave, and Summer Rose just had to say something to him. She had enjoyed his attention. She wanted to know more about him. She wanted to know who he was. Because she could think of nothing better to say, she said, "What is your name?"

The well-dressed man said to her, "Mr. Wonder."

She said, "I don't believe you. That sounds like a made-up name."

The man tilted up his hat, and for the first time Summer Rose could see his face unobstructed. He was quite handsome, and his race, like hers, was mysterious. He could be black, Puerto Rican, Indian or even Dominican. But he was an older man, perhaps in his thirties or even forties. He reached into his jacket and took out the wallet that Summer Rose was quite familiar with, for it had contained the money that she now wore in her garter. The man flipped open his driver's license. His name was J. K. Wonder.

She said, "I'm sorry, but it sounded like a made-up name."

Mr. Wonder said, in an elegant, refined voice, "I gave you all of that money for two reasons, Summer Rose. First, I was at a table earlier, where the dancers were not as attractive as you. I heard them plotting to assault you in the parking lot when you went home tonight, to disfigure you so that you could not dance for tips anymore."

Summer Rose was amazed and chilled by this revelation, but she believed it to be true because she had seen the unfriendly looks on the other dancers' faces and felt the coldness in their dealings with her.

"Second," Mr. Wonder said, "I saw you and I was immediately attracted to you. I don't know why. It's not because you are beautiful, which you certainly are, but I have seen many beautiful women before. You have another quality that I cannot put my finger on. I would like to spend a week with you, watching you dance, until I can identify this mysterious quality of yours."

Summer Rose thought, he wants to fuck me. Don't they all? Although Summer Rose was young, she had lived the life of a woman twice her years. She had gotten pregnant for a thug, who was her lover, the only one she had ever known, and at the same time he was her jailer. He made her dance for tips in clubs to earn money to support his addiction to gambling and illegal narcotics. He also used her as bait to set up for muggings the incautious patrons, like Mr. Wonder, who wanted to meet her for sex after they had seen her dance.

"How do you propose we do this?" Summer Rose said, sadly.

Mr. Wonder said, "I will take you away to my private island for a week, where you shall dance for me. I shall pay you twenty of these hundred-dollar bills every day while you are there, and I promise I will figure out this quality of yours."

"A private island?" she said, thinking of the thug she lived with. He would never permit her to go away for a week. Especially with a rich man. Especially with a rich man he could not follow to bop across the head with the butt of his gun. No way. "I don't know if I can do that."

Mr. Wonder laughed. "Oh, I see, you're thinking of your little baby. Well, he can come too. I shall have the nannies prepare a room for him, too."

She was profoundly shocked. "How do you know about my baby?"

Mr. Wonder laughed. "I just guessed," he said. "I am offering you two thousand dollars a day for seven days, and you turned it down. Certainly, it couldn't be because there is someone here that you love. Of course, you must have a child. Why else would you turn down fourteen thousand dollars?"

When he spoke the amount, her heart fluttered. It was so much money. Fourteen thousand was enough for her to start a new life...thug free. Indeed, she left the club that morning with a lot on her mind.

The thug said, "No. Absolutely not. A rich guy like that has too much security. There would be no way for me to get to the island before he took advantage of you. We have to hit him here. It's the only way. You say his name is Wonder? Like Stevie Wonder? I never heard of him, but I can look it up. We'll set him up right here, and whammo! We'll be rich."

She said, "But he might not have any money on him if we hit him here. Rich guys don't just walk around with wads of money on them, you know? They keep their money in banks. But on that island, he said he's going to give it to me in cash."

The thug scratched his scraggily beard. "I don't know. I just don't know about this." He looked at Summer Rose for assurance.

Summer Rose touched the hundred-dollar bills stacked on the table. It was close to three thousand dollars that Mr. Wonder had tipped her that night. "This guy is no joke. You will take this money he gave me tonight, rent a boat, and you will come to that island and bop him across the head. It will be the easiest fourteen thousand dollars you ever earned."

"I don't know, I don't know, I don't know," the thug said. He was suspicious. She had tried once before to leave him. She was a crafty one. He reached into her blouse for her big breast and pinched her nipple hard. "These are my tiddies, you hear me? Mine."

"I hear you," she whimpered.

He pinched harder. "He touch you, I swear I'll fucking kill you both."

"He won't touch me, I promise," she said, and he released her and she began to rub her nipple to soothe pain. "Junior will be there."

He exploded. "Junior? No way! I'm not letting my son go. That's my boy. No way!"

She calmly explained, "Junior is our insurance. I will stall this guy until you get there. Soon as I get there, I will call you on the cellphone and tell you exactly where the island is. It's somewhere here in Florida. Fisher Island. Star Island. Somewhere in the Keys. One of them. No matter what he asks me to do, I'll hold on to Junior and say that he's nervous being in a new place, and can we wait a few more minutes, please, Mr. Wonder? He has nothing to fear. He'll fall for it. Then you'll show up and bop him across the head, and we're rich."

That was the plan, and the thug fell for it.

Mr. Wonder met Summer Rose and Junior later that day in the parking lot of the strip club. They were transported in his limousine to the airport, where they boarded a private jet that flew them to his island, one of many he owned, ten thousand miles away, in the South Pacific, as they had planned.

For seven days, Summer Rose danced for Mr. Wonder. For seven days, he gazed upon her naked body with quiet fascination. Not once did he touch her, nor did he ask her to touch him. He seemed satisfied simply to watch her. Each night before she went to bed, he gave her two thousand dollars in a wad of twenty hundreds tied with a red ribbon.

On the seventh day before she went to bed, she found next to her stack of hundreds a note that read, *I have figured out the quality you have that attracted me the first time I saw you. Come to my room to have it revealed. Mr. Wonder.*

And Summer Rose thought, well, here it is. Surely, he is going to fuck me now. These rich men are so predictable.

But the truth was, she had fallen in love with him, and she wanted very much for him to return her love. All week, she had followed him around the island, thinking about it, imagining it, wishing for it. He was so beautiful and so good. She had never met a man like that before. At night, after she had danced for him, she would lie in bed rubbing herself, imagining him loving her until she fell asleep.

When she got to his room, he was fully dressed, though she was not. She stood naked at the foot of his bed, upon which he reclined in his silk pajamas. He said, noting her nakedness, "Have you come to dance some more? We are finished for tonight, aren't we?"

Covering her beautiful black breasts with her hands, she stammered, "But I thought…but I thought. Well, you don't want to sleep with me?"

Mr. Wonder said, "Of course, I do, but I would never take advantage of you. When I do sleep with you, it shall be because you want to sleep with me, too. And it will not be sleep, it will be love. We will make love. If not, then I don't want it. You're beautiful, but that is not enough. I must have love."

She was stunned by Mr. Wonder's words as much as by what she spied through the window behind him. It was the thug, approaching the bedroom stealthily. Somehow he had made it to the island. He had his gun in his hand. She knew that Mr. Wonder's personal bodyguard had been dismissed for the evening as he always was. Even the nannies were away, in another house on the island babysitting Junior, with whom they had fallen in love. There was no one to protect Mr. Wonder from the thug except for her. She shouted a warning as the thug aimed the gun, and she threw herself on Mr. Wonder, knocking him flat on the bed. The bullet intended for him went into her side.

Howling in a lover's anguish, the thug jumped through the window and lifted her limp body in his arms, for in his own way, he had loved her. Mr. Wonder sprang up. He wrestled her body away from the thug and knocked him to the ground. Then Mr. Wonder clutched his beloved Summer Rose to his chest and wept terrifically. But the thug jumped up and pulled her away again. And so, Mr. Wonder and the thug, two men of great physical strength, fought over the wounded body of Summer Rose, who awoke in dumbfounded amazement. She was not mortally wounded. It had only been a flesh wound. The shock had but rendered her unconscious. She watched silently as the men fought over her: the ill mannered thug who had traveled ten thousand miles to get her back; and the cultured rich man who had taken her the same distance, but refused to take advantage of her.

They hit each other hard with their fists and clawed at each other like animals until they were slipping in their own blood on the polished wooden floor. They were completely oblivious of the fact that she had regained consciousness.

After a while, she got up and began to dance, naked as the day she was born, and still they did not notice her, so in love with her they were. Summer Rose danced to the sound of their fighting, danced to the sound of two very different men loving her with all of their might.

She danced. She danced. She had never been so happy.

—The End—

I was so proud of my story. I worked on it and worked on it. I sent it off to twenty magazines. And twenty magazines rejected it. One of them was kind enough to write in the margins of the form rejection letter: *This is sooo anticlimactic. You never mentioned what the quality was that Mr. Wonder found in her. Furthermore, he knew that she had a baby because he had been watching her stretch marks all night as she danced for him. Verisimilitude, please. There is no such thing as a perfect body. I'm curious: what is their race, and WHAT does it have to do with the plot? Why not just make them regular white people?*

Verisimilitude? Smart as I was, I didn't know that one. I had to look that one up.

Another wrote: *An interesting story, but it lacks character development. P.S. How did the thug get to the island? Remember that the first rule of creative writing is Show, Not Tell!!*

None of the other magazines even bothered to comment. I became so depressed that I showed it to Tyrone, who got mad and accused me of cheating on him.

"Who is Mr. Wonderful?" he demanded. "Who is he? And why you call me a thug? I know the thug is me. Look how you treat me. I ain't nothin to you. I'm just a piece of shit to you. This how you treat me. Every chance you get, you dig into me. You dig, you dig, you dig." In desperation, I showed it to the lesbian, who loved it.

"It's about me and you, ain't it? Why be so coy? Just change their ethnicity to Puerto Rican and be done with it. Just change them all to womyn. She's living with her life partner, a tough dyke, and this rich bi-sexual femme seduces her and takes her to her island paradise. That would be cool. That would work for me. And don't forget to let her get some nookie on the side from those exotic island girls. That would be hot," she said. "Don't cry. Don't cry, Cindique."

She held me in her arms, Rose, Rosa, Rosita, Rosie, the tattoo artist who had etched her rose on my body and in my heart. I continued to cry.

"*Ay pobrecita!* Don't cry. Don't cry."

I continued to believe in princes and princesses and that happily ever after kind of stuff.

That castle of gold.

# One for the Holy Ghost

On the other hand, sometimes I'm not so optimistic.

Here I am trying to remain inconspicuous in the grocery store across the street and down the road from the hotel, in a loud, sunshine yellow tourist T-shirt and shorts, having ditched my own clothes in the bathroom. I'm wearing dark shades over my eyes and a baseball cap with the brim pulled down to my eyelashes that I've just purchased off the miscellaneous rack at the front of the grocery store, and I'm thinking about the dumb, dumb move I just made.

Obviously, Tyrone had been following Red and me from at least since we left the apartment. Obviously, he had come into the hotel after Red had left and after I had paid for my room and then gone into the gift shop. He had presented his ID showing his last name was the same as mine and convinced the ditzy front desk clerk that he was my husband and he needed to know which room I had registered *us* in. The security guard had gone up there to show him the way to *our* room.

Or perhaps the guard had seen Tyrone up there hanging out in the hall and wondered about it, and then Tyrone had sweet talked him, blah, blah, blah, I'm waiting for my wife, and the security guard had bought it and said, oh, hey, is that her getting off the elevator? Waving at innocent little, dumb, dumb me getting off the elevator. Which meant that Tyrone couldn't just go bounding down the stairs to cut me off before the elevator hit the first floor because that would have alerted the guard that Tyrone's story had not been on the up and up. Then,

Mr. So Cool Tyrone would have taken his time going down the stairs, perhaps in the company of the portly and slightly suspicious security guard. Then he would have exited the hotel and looked around outside and realized that there were just too many places for me to hide. Too many streets to go down. Too many businesses to duck into.

After a while he would have simply given up looking for me and left. The man has no persistence at all. He never sticks with what he starts. One day he was gonna be a police officer, joined the academy—three weeks later he had quit. Then he was gonna be a fire fighter, joined the academy, and two weeks later, he came home wearing a tall, white chef's hat. A new plan. Oh, and think about all the free food. Then it was truck-driving school. Then selling cars. Then a reefer man. Then construction work. No, Tyrone would not look for me too long before giving up.

In fact, I could have bought a pair of cheap binoculars from the drugstore next door to the grocery store and had some good fun watching from across the street as Tyrone walked from one end to the other of the hotel parking lot looking for me, for like two minutes, then gave up and drove off in his Mustang. That is, if I hadn't spotted his Mustang in the last row of cars in the hotel parking lot as I was making my escape. That is, if I hadn't had those scissors in my bag. That is, if I hadn't punctured his tires.

All four of them.

Now he has no way to leave. He is guarding the entrance of the grocery store. I can see him through the glass front. He knows I am in here. He will not leave. This time, he will persist. He has a plan. He has a good plan this time. If he enters the store through one door, I will dash out the other. He is biding his time until the store closes and I have to come out.

My cellphone is packed in a box of my personal stuff at Joan's. The payphones are all near the front entrance. I'm sure an assistant manager will let me use the store phone. It's too tricky to call a cab then try to get past Tyrone without him grabbing me, or hitting me. I will call the police. He'll be in serious trouble. But he can make it ugly. Complicate things. I'll have to explain why I slit his tires. Why I carved him up. He can make me look like the bad guy without trying too hard. Then there will be court. Of course, I'll win. Eventually. I certainly won't be leaving town for a while. But I have to think about my safety. Safety is my first priority. Tyrone's leaving me no choice but to call the police.

Again.

I sneak over to the grocery store's deli, hunker down low at one of the tables, and watch as outside Tyrone presses his face against the glass, searching for me.

There is the chop, chop of the deli lady portioning the large sleeve of salami with a butcher knife. I hunker lower. Chop, chop. I'm thinking. Chop. Remembering.

He used to lock me in the closet.

For days.

He knew that from a child, I was afraid of the dark. It wasn't the hunger or the lack of water and space. It was the lack of light. The lack of seeing what is there. Our building in the rundown Carol City section of Miami was old and constructed of crumbling masonry. There were holes in the wall inside the closet. Like someone had kicked, or punched them there. Some of them so big that things could live inside. There were mice. We never saw them, but we would hear them at night. It sounded like they were coming from inside the closet. He would unscrew the light bulb in there and lock me in the closet for three days. One for the Father. One for the Son. One for the Holy Ghost.

He did it because I was smart. I was always writing things. Learning things. I had been an honors student. I could have graduated and gone to college and become something. I shouldn't be wasting my life like this, stripping in sleazy clubs and being beat on and having the police come to the apartment all the time for all the screaming and shouting. Everyone kept saying I should enroll at the junior college. No one ever said that about him. And so he would lock me away. Mrs. Lassiter found out and called the police on him. He was bad, but he was my bad. I lied to protect him. The beatings got harder. Bounce. Bounce. Bouncing me off the walls. More trips to the closet. The closet was the worst. Mrs. Lassiter had always said in class, "In order to grow, you must learn to face your fears."

I was ready to grow.

I was ready to go.

When he found me with the financial aid application for the junior college, he just about lost his mind. Back to the closet. In the darkness. With the crumbling holes. With the tears. With the things that I could not see. The things that scurried over my legs. That kissed my face when I tried to sleep.

After three days, he tried to open the door to release me.

It would not open.

I had hooked it closed with the arms of his extra large denim jacket. He said, Cindique? You in there? You can come out now. Again he pulled against the door. Cindique? You okay? I didn't answer. I went right on eating my sandwich and drinking from my thermos that I had stashed in the metal lunchbox in there for just in case. Cindique, he said. Open this goddamned door before I break it. I said, and the landlady's gonna make you pay to fix it! He said, fuck you. And he went away. Cheap bastard. If you really love me, break down the goddamned door. What's money where love is concerned? I'm in the dark for you. I'm with the mice for you! You dummy! You punk ass! No answer from him. I continued eating the food I had stashed. Then I turned on the flashlight and finished writing *Summer Rose*.

In the first draft, I called her name Cindique.

I still loved love.

I still loved him, my big dumb thug.

I stayed in there for another night before I came out. I could have stayed longer. I had rations for a week, but I figured Tyrone had suffered enough. And the smell was getting to me. From then on, it was me who ran to the closet when things got ugly. He would sit at the door pleading with me to come out, and me daring him to break down the door. Cheap bastard. Coward. Show your love. Half the time I didn't use the flashlight. In the darkness there is light. In the darkness, I learned to see. In the darkness, I learned the thing I was afraid of became less scary when I stopped running away and faced it head on.

That's why I got so much attitude these days.

That's why I can admit that even now I still have feelings for Tyrone, shitty as that sounds. That's why I can admit that maybe he knows this and is feeding off it. When he walked out, it was me who had pleaded, don't lose the key, baby, I won't change the lock.

No. I'm not gonna call the police. I have to face Tyrone. He screwed up and ran off, but now he's come back like I asked him to. He wants me back. He knows I want him, too. I've only been with one man since he ran off…

Pining.

Bounce.

But I know one thing for sure, it's not gonna be like it was before. It can't be. I can't go back to that.

I take a deep breath and rise from my chair at the deli table. The deli lady is finished chopping and she smiles at me, in her white hat and apron, her fleshy arms, can I help you? But I don't have a smile for her. My manners are gone. I'm all attitude now. I'm thinking about Tyrone. If he wants to talk, we will talk. If he can make me feel like wanting to follow him up to that hotel room with its king sized bed, then I will go. Yeah. But if he wants to play it like the dark, old closet days, my hand's already in my bag on the sturdy scissors.

I'll hem some more of his goddamned pants for him, if he wants to play it like dat.

# I Got Your back

The tall, thin man strides toward my table from the dairy aisle wearing a bright yellow T-shirt and shorts. It is the silliest outfit I have ever seen, second only to the one I am presently wearing. In fact, it is identical to the one I am presently wearing. I fly into Red's waiting arms. Kiss him all over his face and lips. "Thank you, Red. Thank you, thank you."

His eyes twinkle, his smile curls upward. "You did a good job on his tires," he says.

"You saw that?"

"He almost caught you. He saw you doing it. That security guard was with him, or he would've caught you. He was right behind you, and you out there taking your la-dee-da time cutting his tires. Damn, you're hardcore. Remind me not to mess with you."

"He was right behind me." Kiss face. Kiss face.

"And I was right behind him," Red says. He has a young man's face. A baby face. He is skinny. But he is a man, and the way he says it, he wants me to know it. He's no punk. He removes the baseball cap from my head and brushes my hair back with his fingers, tenderly. "He wasn't gonna get too far if he had jumped at you. Not with me standing there. Don't you worry about that."

I say, "Not with you there."

I cling to his chest.

He rubs my back.

"I know he's your man and all, but he's kind of a punk. He stayed in his car until I left the hotel. I was watching him to see what he would do. I figured he was your husband, but I wasn't sure," Red says. "I was like, who is this brother following us for the last ten miles? No matter where we turned, he turned. Then he swung into that hotel, too? Naw, that was kinda suspicious. And while we were talking, he was just sitting in that car. Waiting. Watching you. I'm like, naw, this is really suspicious. You went in the hotel, and I had a bad feeling about it. And yep, he got out of the car. A big brother. Pumped."

"With twisty hair?"

"No neck?"

"That's my Tyrone."

Red chuckles. "You must like brothers with wild hair," he says, running a hand over his own clean-shaved head. "But he wouldn't go inside while I was there. He just stood by the car, kinda looking off to the side, and I'm like, naw, naw, naw. This has to be my imagination. Stuff like this only happens in the movies. Give the brother some slack. So I pretended to leave to see what he would do. When I checked my rearview mirror, bingo! Brother was making tracks running inside that hotel. So I came back. Spotted you in the little gift shop buying these fine, fine clothes."

Red tugs playfully at my ugly yellow T-shirt. I tug at his.

"But at that point I still wasn't sure it was him. So I ducked back out and told one of the security guards to help me find my friend Tyrone who was somewhere in this hotel looking for me. The guard said, Tyrone? Him and his wife Cindique done checked in upstairs on the 6$^{th}$ floor, but he don't have a key. He don't know where she at either. I'll go tell him you're here looking for him."

"You sent the guard." Kiss cheek. Kiss cheek. "Thank you."

"Yeah. So now I knew it was him, but by the time I got back to the gift shop, you were gone."

"I was going up in the elevator."

"You were coming *down* in the elevator—and running through that lobby in your fine, fine clothes. I was like, Cindique done seen a ghost or something," he says. "Next thing I know, old Tyrone and the security guard are huffing down the stairs. Tyrone is telling him something like, she need to take her medicine, officer. I gotta give her her medicine. I gotta catch up with her. And the security guard is like, well we can just call her name on the P.A., there's no running in the hotel, sir. Be careful you don't slip and fall. What a trip. And I was right behind 'em."

"You were right behind them," I say. "Thank you for having my back."

He blushes. "It's all good. The Bronco's out back."

I look beyond Red to the front of the store. Tyrone is still out there. Tyrone looks down and checks his watch. Red has me by the hand, and he's leading me to the back of the store, through the produce section, beyond the restrooms, to the loading area. We pass through a large staging warehouse where workers in coveralls and safety harnesses are unloading cardboard crates of Kellogg's Cornflakes from a truck. The workers are friendly. One of them waves and says, "Y'all looking for empty boxes? Y'all can take as many as you like. A few of 'em already stacked up over there if you like." He points to a stack of flattened boxes and then goes back to unloading the truck.

Red leads me to a loading bay that empties into the service alley. His Bronco is parked a few feet away. He lets go of my hand and hops down into the alley, then reaches up and lifts me down. He carries me to the Bronco like a bride over the threshold. He is a tall, wiry man with gentle hands. He is no gingerbread. He is a strong man.

"Here we are, madam," he says, setting me down next to the passenger door, which he opens with a click of his remote key.

But I have a one track mind. He walks around and gets into the driver's seat before he notices that I'm still standing outside the Bronco. He powers down the window. "Whuzzup? Get in before that crazy, no-neck fool thinks about checking around the back."

I stick my head inside the window. "Truth for truth."

"Aw, no." Red scrunches up his face. "Let's go please. I don't want no trouble from Tyrone if I can avoid it."

"A relationship has to be based on honesty, you agree?"

"I agree, but—."

"And I'm liking you, and you're liking me, right?"

"Yeah. I'm liking you, Cindique, though you are trying me. You are really trying me."

"If I get in this car with you, we're probably gonna start some kinda relationship, right?"

"Yeah. I'm feeling real good about you. I'm liking you big time. I'm thinking how much I'm gonna be missing you when you leave to go upstate."

I am touched. I say, "Things like that can be worked out. Things like that aren't written in stone, right?"

He nods. "You don't *have* to move up there."

"Oh, yes. I definitely have to move up there. I can't stay here anymore, Red. There's too much of my past down here."

"Or, well, I could maybe move up there too, uhm, I mean if it comes to that. Things aren't written in stone."

"You will move up there with me. You will. Won't you?"

"I will," he says. "Because I'm really liking you big time."

"Then we have a serious problem on our hands because what you just described is a relationship, and a relationship has to be based on honesty," I say. "The truth won't kill you, Red, it's the lies that kill you."

He grunts, "Whatever." He reaches across the seat and pushes open the door. He spits out a sudden string of curse words and says, "Get in the car, Cindique. Okay? Yes. Yes. I'm fucking Joan Darcy."

When I step up into the Bronco and close the door, it is suddenly very chilly.

# PART V

▼

# Today, You Have Come Into My Life

"Well?"

His hand is over his mouth. His voice sounds disembodied in the dark interior of the car. "Want me to put on some music, or something?"

"Just finish it."

He looks straight ahead into the dark alleyway. "It's over between us. Now. After this, I mean I'm gonna end it for permanent, but...she's a beautiful woman, not at all like you think she is. This whole thing with you staying at her house is for real. That's the kind of good person she is. I'm glad you're seeing that side of her. The people at work, they don't know her. They don't know she's an orphan. They don't know she grew up on the streets in Romania. She has a soft side. She loves animals and children. She gives to the church. She pays her tithes. The people at work, they think she's like what you called her. Groan of Arc. That wasn't very nice. From the first day you came to work, she liked you. She said you reminded her of her daughter, who's dead. She was black. Her sons up at college are black, too. She adopted them. See what I mean? You don't know her. I mean, that's why she put you with me. Because I'm the best. Because she wanted me to train you. She liked you. She would have done anything for you. She's down with black people. But you started calling her Groan of Arc...why did you do that? She never did anything to you. Groan of Arc? Joan of Darkness? What was that all about?"

"I'm sorry, Red. I don't know what to tell you. She was the boss, and my head was in a bad place. I was trying to be funny."

"I thought you were so cute when you first came to work, that very first day I was digging you real tight, I was like, oh man, she's hot, but I pulled back when you started calling her that shit."

"I feel real crappy about that." I find his hand in the dark and whisper to him, "I didn't know, Red. I didn't know."

He brushes it off. "What happened between me and Joan, what has been happening, is that her husband at this point in his life would rather be with some other woman. And I would rather be with someone who loves me. No matter how old, or what color. I can't say that I love her. I can't say that I ever loved her. In that way. But she was a friend I could turn to when things in my life weren't going so hot. It's not like I could talk to my parents about these kinds of things. She understood. And she started turning to me, too. We would stay at McDarc hours after it had closed, just talking…about how we were being hurt by the ones who loved us. No woman wants to be dumped. It makes her feel old. Ugly. She knows why he spends so much time away at the other branches. She knows what's going on. Me and Joan would hold onto each other and find the strength we needed to make it to the next day. One night it was raining…I don't want to get into this, you know how these things happen, but she told me she liked the sound of the rain. I said, yeah, it's nice. She said, Alexandros used to like to watch me dance naked in the rain. I said, that must have been beautiful. She said, when I was young I was beautiful, and I danced in the rain for Alexandros. I said, you are still beautiful. She began to cry, and I held her. She said, I am not beautiful. I said, but you are. And she said, you are beautiful. You have such beautiful skin. I said, thank you. And she kissed me…I don't want to get into this. You'll only misunderstand. She's not like that. I'm not like that. We were not going to have sex. We were just going to be there for each other. We needed each other. The sex just kinda grew out of it in a strange way. A nice way. Our clothes didn't even come off, we were just sorta comforting. Hugging and holding. Kissing. I was in her before I realized it. She was sorta on my lap, I was in a chair. I don't remember thinking, wow, this is my boss, wow, this is a white woman, wow, let me see what her tits look like, or nothing like that. I don't remember stroking or coming. I just remember the holding. The tears. I just remember the comforting. And that it felt right. That it was raining. It was not about sex…the point is, for the past six months, seven, we have been each other's support. We both know that it's not leading anywhere. We both promised that if the right person came along for either of us, the other would end it without pettiness. We both promised that we would be strong, no matter what we felt, and resist the damned pettiness. We don't belong to each other, what the hell else could we promise? So yes, I am fucking Joan Darcy. Was fucking Joan Darcy. Did fuck her last night…and told her goodbye…and today is a new day. Today, you have come into my life," he says. "And that's the truth."

# MISSISSIPPI

"Truth for truth."

It is dark in the Bronco, except for the glow-in-the-dark stripes outlining the dashboard instruments. Red lifts my hand and brushes it against his lips. "Can we just go, baby? The grocery store's about to close. Tyrone ain't as stupid as you think."

"Truth for truth," I repeat, withdrawing my hand.

"I told you all the truth that I have."

"The picture of your little boy in the cubicle is very cute. But he's dark. Tawana, you said, is lighter than you, and you are red, Red. How can two very fair people have a dark child?"

"I lied," he says, starting the engine. "But the truth is ugly."

I buckle my seatbelt. "It's not too hard to figure. She crept on you. Your baby's not your baby."

Red manages to laugh a tense, high laugh. "No. That boy is mine. That's one of the few things in this world I'm sure of." Red shakes his head.

I shake mine, too. "I know you love him and all, and that's great. I mean, in this day and age to find a father who loves his son—a father who would marry some girl he knocked up to be with his son, but you need to stop all that church boy shit. Don't be a fool no more for that crazy girl. I don't want to get all up in your business, but I ain't no fool either. Open your eyes. The boy is dark."

"He's dark because Tawana's dark," Red says.

"She's dark?"

"She's dark…but beautiful. The baby got his skin from her. Tawana is dark. Everything else I said about her is true, though."

"You liar!"

"Sorry."

I'm shivering with rage. "Liar, liar. Oh, you are a liar."

"—real sorry."

Shivering. Okay, so now this dark, *but* beautiful girl from Mississippi is the mother of his child, is his ex-wife, is his cousin. Naw. Something's still blurred. Something's still not right with the picture. I grumble, "So then, the white man she went to meet that night, he's not her father? Who was he if he's not her father?"

A frown is the answer to my question.

"Red, you is a lyin mofo, you know that?"

Red puts the Bronco in drive, and the car begins to roll forward.

"With your lyin red ass!"

Shivering. But in a way, it's kinda good, too. I like that Tawana is dark as me. Maybe darker. What can I say? I have good skin, a smooth complexion, but I am dark. Like mama. She used to tell me, "Don't worry. When you get married, you can find a nice light-skinned man to raise your color and give you pretty children." I don't like to think about color. I don't like to think about color at all. I say to Red, "Damn. Just say it. The white man she met in the rundown neighborhood was her boyfriend from Mississippi, right?"

The car bumps across the broken asphalt of the service alley past the back entrances of the grocery store, the drugstore, a gym, a bakery. There are many flattened cardboard boxes neatly stacked back here for anyone who needs them. "Yes, he was her boyfriend from Mississippi," Red says. "The same guy she's living with now. You little private eye."

"Any fool can figure that. He had come down to meet her because he had missed her."

"Yes, he had missed her. He had come down to meet her."

"She must've missed him, too. She spent an hour in there fucking him. With her slutty ass self."

"No, don't call her that," he says. "Yes. She spent an hour in there fucking him. But I loved her, Cindique. I told her it was wrong what she was doing. I preached to her. I prayed for her."

"Your own cousin."

"Fourth cousin."

We roll out of the service alley, and Red turns the corner into the main parking lot. We both look, and way off at the far end, in front of the grocery store, we see Tyrone leaning on a shopping cart, waiting. If I weren't so mad at Red, I would have found it kinda funny and laughed. If Red weren't so caught up in his lies, he might have laughed too at Tyrone checking his watch and pressing his face against the glass. What did I ever see in Tyrone? I must have been out of my mind chasing after something like that. I don't need him. He needs me. Big baby. We rumble through the parking lot and the Bronco pulls out onto the main road.

Red's voice is flat when it comes back. "I preached to her in the car that night. I tried to get her to see the light, and she seduced me." A light rain is falling now, and the wipers are sweeping across the wet glass. Rhythmically. "She started crying. She said she was in pain. Real pain. I said, holy ghost pain? She said, no, chest pain. Pain in my chest. She said, my chest is hurting. My chest is hurting bad. My chest is hurting. Will you rub it for me, cousin? Please rub it for me, Cousin Roderick. I can trust you, Cousin Roderick, like I can't trust anybody else. Cause you're a Christian, Cousin Roderick, I can trust you to rub it for me...yeah, she seduced me. Oh she seduced me real good."

"And you liked it. You liked fucking your cousin."

"It's not like that, Cindique. I swear. I was born again. I lost everything I believed in—my faith, my family."

"But at least you had her."

"At least I had her," he echoes. "For a while. Three years. We were happy, completely happy, for three years. He tried, but she was resisting him. I thought she had broken free of him and his wickedness." Red really steps on the gas. He says, "Sometimes when we talk, I think we still have a chance. That it can still work. The Bible says that you can't be divorced from your first love—."

"Stop it. Stop it. You're just making a fool out of yourself. He never gave her up. Maybe she never gave him up. Slow down please."

My hand is on his hand on the wheel.

"It's not your fault, Red."

"My fault? I thought you had figured it out, Detective Columbo."

A macho sniffle. Hand over his nose. Red is a mess. Driving too fast. The rain coming down hard now against the glass. The wipers on low not helping much. Red turns the wipers on high and puts his hand over his mouth, muffling his words:

"The boyfriend is her stepfather."

"Oh...shit."

# GROANING

"I was trying to tell her you can't go around fucking your stepfather. I was trying to tell her it's a sin. How did I end up fucking her? How? She ruined my whole life—."

"Red."

"I wish I could rub inside your pants like I do for my stepdad. I wish I could sit on your lap with my panties off like I do for my stepdad. Me and my daddy, me and my daddy. He likes it. He likes it a whole lot—."

"Red!"

Red is groaning, the car is swerving. The squeacha, squeacha, squeacha, squeacha of the wipers on high.

"Red. Red. Stop the car, Red. Red, please. There's a gas station."

He swings into the gas station and pulls up at the pumps. Shuts off the engine. Covers his face with his hands. "It's so fucked up."

"Poor Tawana."

"—so fucked up—."

"Yucky—."

"—so fucked up—."

"Damn. Damn. Mmm…but what you need to do is move on with your life. What you need to do is get your boy away from that mess."

"Yeah. I been thinking about that. I been—."

"I'm real sorry for Tawana, and all, but he don't need to grow up in that mess. It just ain't right. When we get settled, that's the first thing we need to take care of. We need to get that boy out of there."

"Yeah." Red looks up. Says, from deep in his throat, "He's six years old."

"He's so cute."

"Yes, he is," Red says. His voice reviving. "He knows it, too. You should see him. He's gonna be a lady killer when he grows up. You watch."

"What's his name?"

"Ezekiel Roderick Redd, Jr."

"Your first name is Ezekiel?"

"Sad but true. They used to call me Zeke growing up. I hated it. It sounded too country."

"But Zeke is a nice name. I think it's cool." My face is against his neck. I touch his face lightly with my hand. Around his eyes and cheeks is still damp. "I like it."

"You like it?" He looks at me. Hopeful.

"Yeah." I kiss him on his cheek. It is salted with tears.

"Then you can call me Zeke." Red offers his lips. I like the way he kisses. I like the way he pulls at my lips when we kiss.

His lips taste like tears.

# UNDER THE SPREADING
# SEA GRAPE TREE

"I'm glad I met you."

"I'm glad I met you."

"You're just saying that to be nice."

"The way you made me come today, now that was being nice."

"You're a mess," says Ezekiel Roderick Redd, Sr., who laughs, slows the car, leans over, and kisses me again. "And don't forget, funny lady, you made me come, too."

"Boys always come."

"It's not everyday they get to come with somebody who cares about them. Somebody they love."

"Did you say *love?*"

He lifts his head and points. "Over there. That's where Joan lives."

Millionaires row on the Atlantic side of Key Biscayne. In the landscape lighting, the estates appear dotted with coco plum hedges, sea grape trees, leaning palms, tennis courts, swimming pools, and here and there beyond it all, rise the long masts of yachts. Hers is an Early Victorian mansion on three acres of land, its lighted majesty reflecting off the black mirror of the Atlantic at night. The picturesque white cottage beside the house, I assume, is my temporary residence. The cottage has its own garage. And satellite dish. There is movement inside. The help, making final preparations for my arrival.

"Sweet," I say, as we pull into the expansive driveway, the tires crunching deliciously on the gravel as they come to rest.

"Wait till you get inside. The place is incredible."

"I imagine."

He kills the engine. I squeeze his hand. I look into his eyes.

He says, "You're getting all mushy."

"You make me mushy. I'm seriously digging you right now."

"Wait'll we get inside."

"I got Red on the brain."

"Calm down, Cousin Tawana." Chuckling.

"Don't make me have to snap on you, John the Baptist. Don't make me have to stab all the tires on this damned Bronco. You know I'll do it."

"Then Joan'll be really pissed. She bought it for me."

"Oh snap. I should've known. That bitch better not be buying my man no more toys."

"No more toys. I promise."

"Just because she has more money than me don't mean I won't go off on her Key Biscayne living ass."

"I know. I know." Red whistles. "Oh yeah. This is gonna work. We're gonna be good together. Fuckin and fightin like we do." He looks at me all sly. "Of course, we got a few things to work out first."

"Like what?"

"Truth for truth."

My hands are on my hips. "Huh? You think this is a problem for me? This is *not* a problem for me. I ain't scared. I ain't got nothin to hide. What do you want to know?"

"Jake. The pornographer."

"Don't call him that. He's not that anymore. He owns an insurance company now."

"Well, good for him," Red says. "But I don't know—all of those things he did to you with his tongue. Don't you see he was a pervert? You were a child—you were naive. He was so afraid to put his penis in you, so afraid to go to jail for robbing the cradle. A pornographer? I'm not buying it."

"Jake kept his promise. He was a good, kind, gentle, and honorable man."

"Sticking his face in a fifteen-year-old's coochie."

"He might have licked the cradle, but he didn't rob it."

"You swear? Come on now, you can be honest with me. I was honest with you."

"I said truth for truth, didn't I? For real. Jake was a good man."

"All right, baby. Let's not fight about it. I believe you," he says, laughing, kissing me on the forehead. And that is that.

The night air is fresh and a little bit cool after the rain as we get out of the car and walk toward the cottage holding hands. There's the smell of the ocean breeze and the fragrance of roses, which proliferate in the landscaping of Joan's estate. It's exciting. The newness of this thing. The freshness. It can work with me and Red. My head is filled with visions of us in the future. I will turn 21 in his arms. 31. 41. The loving, the playing, the building of a life together. The honesty. It's all new, but we have a good chance because we are honest. We believe in castles of gold. We arrive at the cottage hand in hand, and I hear him say kind of under his breath: "I'm a good man, too. I mean, I know I got problems, but I try my best."

"You're the best," I say, clutching his hand tighter. "The best."

I reach up and find his lips, my good man. My prince in freckled armor. We stand outside the cottage near a low hedge and an ironwork bench under a spreading sea grape tree. There is the piney smell from the cypress mulch that crunches under our feet as we kiss. But I can't go through with it. Despite his skills as a telephone solicitor, he's so naïve. He's still a church boy underneath, really. I can't do it to him. I can't.

I say to him: "Technically speaking."

"Hmm?"

"Technically speaking, Jake did not rob the cradle. The legal age is 18 in Florida, and Jake did not touch me in that way in Florida. But when he took me down to the Bahamas, he rocked it hard all day."

"Rocked it hard—." Red's eyes blaze. "You lied to me."

I laugh, jabbing him playfully in the ribs. "Technically I did not lie. Technically he did not rob the cradle because in the Bahamas the cradle ends at 14."

Red is not smiling. Not frowning.

"Red? Red?"

Red sits down on the ironwork bench and pulls me across his lap. I'm cracking up with laughter as he tries to spread me across his lap. I will not keep still. I will not. "Stop! Stop!" I say. Writhing.

He raises his hand. "Technically speaking," he says, waiting until I've gotten a good look at his raised hand, "I am not going to spank you."

"Help! Help! Child abuse! I'm underage."

"Screaming ain't gonna help you."

"Boo-hoo! Boo-hoo!" I say, cracking up with laughter. Inside the cottage, the shadows move. The help look out the windows at us, frown, shake their heads, and go back to work preparing my rooms. I confess to Red: "But I like being spanked when I'm naughty. I forgot to tell you. It gets me so hot."

"Well, there you have it. Technically, this is not a spanking. Technically it's foreplay." He applies his hand to my booty several times very hard. His gray eyes smile down at me.

Truth for truth, I have never been spanked before, but it feels very, very good. It seems like something I can get into if my man likes it. It's all playful. It's all loving. It's all good. Anything that Ezekiel Roderick Redd, Sr. does to me feels good. This ain't mama. This ain't Tyrone. This is my prince.

Truth for truth, I'm no fool, and Red ain't one either.

This is the beginning of a relationship that could easily fail. He could slip back to Cousin Tawana land. I could become impatient. Outgrow him.

Slip back to Tyrone and his shitty, familiar ways.

But I believe in castles of gold and so does Red, and if we work at it we just might find ourselves old, fat, and happy together. Mr. and Mrs. Prince Charming.

After about a minute, he stops spanking and I follow him into the cottage on Joan's property, where he finishes the job.

Then it's my turn to do him.

Bounce.

The world is just a big red bouncing ball of fun, y'all.

I'm gonna be Mrs. Cindique Sanders-Redd soon. I'm gonna live happily ever after.

Bounce. Bounce.

# PART VI

# TRUTH FOR TRUTH

Bounce.

Bounce.

Bounce.

"…Technically I did not lie. Technically he did not rob the cradle because in the Bahamas the cradle ends at 14."

Red is not smiling. Not frowning. At least that part of it was true. But we do not sit and do spanky-spanky on the ironwork chair. I made that part up. You see, Red is jangling the keys to the cottage on Joan's property. Mmmm.

"Red? Red?" Before I know it, my red man has opened the door to the cottage and has carried me across the carpet and set me down on the couch. We start tearing into each other's clothes. "Oh, he's mad now," I say, laughing.

He grins down at me, shaking his head. "Technically speaking. Technically speaking, you're a heathen."

"Oooh, John the Baptist is getting all mad." Pulling off his shirt.

"Oh yeah." Kneeling over me. Pushing up my T-shirt.

"Oooh!"

There is a sound from inside one of the bedrooms, a shadow stretches across the floor, as the help, an aged Cuban woman in a square-collared maid's uniform and her gray hair in a bun under a hairnet, comes out of the bedroom. She fixes her angry, coal black eyes on us, and Red freezes. The woman holds the long handle of a dust mop in front of her like a staff.

From out of the room behind her, steps Joan Darcy.

I pull my T-shirt down over my breasts. Red lets out a heavy sigh. Joan appears tall, thin, and very delicate in her tiny black skirt and slender heels. She is the Romanian orphan today. Standing naked in the storm. She says, "Oh, I'm sorry," then turns away from us, makes for the door, grabbing at the knob twice before grasping it at last and pulling it open. She flings herself outside, like escaping.

"Shit, shit," Red says, hauling on his yellow T-shirt.

"Red."

"Oh, shit." Pulling up his yellow shorts. "I gotta go, Cindique. Oh, shit."

"You'll be back." I find his hand and cling to that. I demand a promise from his eyes. "You'll be right back."

"I gotta explain it to her. I owe her that."

"I should leave?"

"Just stay here. She's not like that. I just gotta explain it to her."

"I'm confused. I'm so confused. You said you had explained it to her. I need to get out of here."

"Just lemme go talk to her, Cindique. Don't do nothin. Just lemme go talk to her."

I do not look at his face as he frees himself from my hand. I do not look at him. I can't look. Oh, Red. Oh, Red. I sense the movement as he scurries after her. I do not ask her to do this, but the woman with the dust mop goes to the door and clicks it closed after him. She comes back and says something to me that I can't make out. She has the dust mop in her hand. She is just the help. She has no right to talk to me this way. I am not crying. She has no right to smell like roses. It's her perfume. Her old lady perfume. My mother's scent. She's saying something to me in bad English. *Why are they so liars? Why are they so machos?*

She has no right. She knows nothing about him. He's not like that at all. He's a good man. He's strong. She knows nothing about him, standing there with her dust mop. The damned help, that's all she is. I resist her with my silence and I do not cry. She goes back in the room, the Cuban lady who smells like my mother, and finishes cleaning a space I will never enter.

I continue to watch through the window as he talks with Joan, without touching her. The smoke of their glowing cigarettes circles above their heads. I hate her short skirt, her long, skinny legs, her white skin. She pretended to be my friend. She pretended to like me. That bitch. She set me up. He's such a fool. Doesn't he see that she's just using him? How far does he think their relationship will go? It can't go very far. She's too old for him. She's married to a rich man. Nasty bitch. I should bust on them. I should tell. I should—. There is a comforting distance between them for the longest while. It disappears when she gets in the Bronco with him and they go somewhere. I do not go into the room that has been prepared for me. I do not cry as I wait on the couch in my ugly yellow shorts and T-shirt. When he finally calls, I am wide awake. Curled up on the couch. Smoking. It's about three in the morning.

"—you can stay there. She has no problem with you staying there. She's a really great person."

"Isn't she, though? I hate her. I fucking hate her."

"—shouldn't say that because she likes you very much and says it's okay for you to stay there till like tomorrow or even the next day because she understands your situation with Tyrone. She was really worried about you. See, she's a really nice person, really."

"I hate you."

"You know how I feel about you, how I'll always feel about you, but right now, I gotta do this thing here because it wouldn't be right to hurt her."

"You're hurting me."

"—she's my friend."

"—hurting me."

"—you know how I feel about you, how I'll always feel about you, but right now—"

"Can you come over at least? Can I see you one more time at least? Can you sneak over? Lemme hold you one more time?"

"It's not possible…maybe when you get upstate."

"I'm not going upstate if you're not coming."

"But she set it up for you—."

"I don't care! I don't care! I need you, Red, I need you. I'm staying right here until you come back to me. You promised."

"Cindique, Cindique, you know how it is."

"Because I'm dark?"

"No! Hell no!"

"Yes it is."

"I owe her."

"Because I'm not your cousin?"

"Stop it, Cindique. Don't do this. This is hard for me. You of all people should understand. You of all people should know why I have to do this. I can't hurt her like this. Not right now. We've been friends too long."

"I'm your friend."

"Not as long as her."

"What!"

"I owe her."

"You used me."

"No, I didn't. I never wanted to hurt you, I never meant to lead you on. I really do feel strong about you, but me and Joan have a relationship. A real relationship. She helps me out with stuff with the baby and Tawana. She helped me with a lawyer when Tawana took me to court. Okay, I'm gonna give it to you straight up. She hooked me up with funds when my commissions were down and it was hard to make the support."

"Oh. You're one of those. That's what you are. Oh damn. Oh damn."

"Naw, it's not like that. That's not how it is, see? She hooked me up when I needed her. She paid my support so Tawana couldn't put me in jail. It took me a long time to pay her back. A long time. And she was real cool about it. Then finally I got good on the phones and paid her back. This was like last month…I haven't always been a superstar phone pro, you know? So if I leave her now, how would that look? It would look like I was just using her. Do you know what she is risking to be with me? You gotta appreciate that."

"You love Tawana. You love Joan. You love everybody but me."

"No, Cindique. I love you, too."

"You dog. You punk. You liar."

"Cindique."

"Liar!"

"Cindique."

"Fuck you, you liar!"

The phone goes dead, and I'm still saying, "You liar! Why couldn't you tell the truth, Red? Why couldn't you just tell the truth? You liar. You liar. You liar."

# BREATHE

The next day, I drive north.

I drive real slow.

The McDarc branch upstate is happy to have a talented phone pro like me. I come highly recommended, thanks to Joan. (Slut.) I don't want her word to stand for anything. (Manipulating bitch.) I have my own two feet to stand on. I show them what I can do. I pick up the phone on the desk without asking permission. The move stuns them. I call and I call, reciting the spiel mechanically, and I make three sales before the interview is over.

They are delighted.

They say that I will make manager in no time. They say that I will bounce back.

Bounce? Now how do they know that?

But, yeah. Yeah.

That's a good plan. That is the plan. But you knew that already because you know how this ends. You know how I am. Nobody can keep you down when your heart is made of rubber.

No matter how much you love him.

Oh, Red. Oh, Red.

**Cindique Sanders**
**December 11**
**Tallahassee, Florida**

# About the Author

Preston L. Allen, a graduate of the University of Florida, received his MFA from Florida International University. He has been published in numerous literary anthologies including Gulfstream, Asili, The Seattle Review, The Crab Orchard Review, DrumVoices 2002, and is the recipient of a State of Florida Individual Artist Fellowship in Literature. He is the winner of the Sonja H. Stone Prize in Literature for Churchboys and Other Sinners (Carolina Wren Press, 2003) and his debut thriller, Hoochie Mama (Writer's Club Press, 2001) was a finalist for the Gold Pen Award. His erotic fiction appears in Brown Sugar (Plume Penguin, 2000) and Brown Sugar 2 (Washington Square, 2002). He lives in Miami, where he teaches creative writing. He can be contacted at pallenagogy@aol.com.

0-595-29871-0

5486677R0

Made in the USA
Lexington, KY
15 May 2010